MW01443369

Sweet Vengeance

Violet S.R. Cox

Sweet Vengeance

Violet S.R. Cox

Violet S.R. Cox

Sweet Vengeance

CONTENT & TRIGGER WARNING

Like most revenge stories, Sweet Vengeance revolves around a girl who is given a second chance and uses it to exact revenge on her ex-boyfriend, who raped and left her for dead. It is a little dark/morbid and may contain some of the following. If you are easily triggered by any of these, please brace yourself. Please read responsibly.

- Rape/ sexual assault
- Explicit sex scenes
- Foul language (Mostly name calling and curse words)
- Parental Neglect and child abuse
- Domestic violence
- General violence
- Blood & Gore
- Detailed Murder
- Death
- PTSD
- Anxiety attacks
- Use of sharp utensils (Including throwing blades, daggers and kitchen knives.)

You have been warned. Please read at your discretion.

Violet S.R. Cox

Sweet Vengeance

DEDICATION

I dedicate this book
To a few beloved pupils, who may be gone, but are never forgotten in our hearts.
My Mom, Papa, Darrell, Jason,
Greg, Sherrill, Bill, Uncle Pork and
Uncle Donald.
Until We Meet Again.

These amazing people taught me so many things over the short years of knowing them. They were always so encouraging and had this bright light that surrounded them. Could make anyone who was around them smile or laugh. They will be missed and forever remembered for their personalities.
Fly high my friends.

***

I also dedicate this book to my fellow Revenge story lovers.
To the readers who love the movies: *Enough, Spit on Your Grave,* and *Sleeping with the Enemy.*

Violet S.R. Cox

Table of Contents

Content & Trigger Warning V
Dedication IX
Chapter *1* 1
Chapter *2* 8
Chapter 3 18
Chapter 4 26
Chapter 5 35
Chapter 6 42
Chapter 7 51
Chapter 8 60
Chapter 9 67
Chapter 10 71
Chapter 11 81
Chapter 12 88
Chapter 13 92
Chapter 14 97
Chapter 15 107
Chapter 16 111
Chapter 17 118
Chapter 18 122
Chapter 19 125

Chapter 20	131
Chapter 21	135
Chapter 22	140
Chapter 23	148
Chapter 24	154
Chapter 25	163
Chapter 26	169
Chapter 27	177
Chapter 28	183
Chapter 29	190
Chapter 30	196
Chapter 31	203
Chapter 32	210
Chapter 33	220
Chapter 34	225
Chapter 35	236
Chapter 36	241
Chapter 37	248
Chapter 38	251

Sweet Vengeance

Violet S.R. Cox

Sweet Vengeance

XIII

CHAPTER 1

The fear and confusion courses through me like a steady flowing stream of water as I run as fast as I can down the abandoned dirt road. Surrounded by nothing but dark trees, the moonlight tries to fight its way through the canopy of branches. The dim glow of the moonlight barely illuminates the dirt road beneath my feet, giving me a creepy feeling; sending rising goosebumps across my arms. The tree branches loom over me, almost like hands reaching out, threatening to snatch me up. The whole scene reminds me of the movie *Wrong Turn*. My eyes dart around frantically, searching desperately for safe refuge.

I keep stumbling over the hem of my long, beautiful, pale blue dress that I spent hours carefully picking out for tonight's special occasion. My hair, which was styled carefully into a glamorous braided bun, now falls loose from its hold as my long, dark mane gradually slips past my shoulders.

I feel like Cinderella running from the Prince at midnight instead of trying to beat my step-sisters and step-mother home. I am running from my prom date—who can't take the word *no* for an answer. The heavy pounding of footsteps behind me tells me he is only a few yards away and closing quickly. My heart is beating hard in my chest, not only from the adrenaline coursing through me but also *fear*.

No one ever turned Abe Smith down. Because all the girls at school wanted to date the quarterback, he was used to girls throwing themselves at him. They were willing to spread their legs for him, almost like bitches in heat.

I wasn't ready or willing to do what he wanted. He was pushing me to do things against my wishes and consent. I didn't want to be just another name on his "I tapped that" list.

We only started dating a couple weeks ago. I didn't know him well enough to be intimate with him in any way.

My bare feet slam onto the hard, uneven ground, occasionally landing on sharp, jagged rocks, causing me to stumble and grimace in pain. My breathing is hard, raspy, and labored as my lungs fight for oxygen. I'm definitely not much of a runner, and I never was. I was always in too much pain to keep up with the others in gym class. The sweat I have worked up caresses my body almost like a forbidden embrace as it clings to my skin.

Even with my best efforts, I start to slow down.

I hear the pounding footsteps only a few feet behind me now. Pushing myself harder, I try to quicken my pace, but he closes the distance almost instantly as his hand wraps around my wrist. His vise grip is strong enough to abruptly stop me and make me slam back into his rock-solid chest like a rubber band being snapped. My back feels as if it has hit a solid brick wall, and I freeze like a deer in headlights; his other hand wraps around my body, slowly creeping upwards. My breathing hitches as fear overtakes me; his hand slides to my throat, pulling me closer.

Sweet Vengeance

"Did you really think you could outrun me, darling?" his gravelly voice asks, sounding amused only inches away from my ear. The warmth of his breath against my neck sends a shiver of dread through my entire body.

His hand on my wrist releases as his other hand tightens around my throat and guides me to face him. He squeezes my neck, causing my hands to fly to his as I feel my oxygen being cut off. The panic seeps deep into my bones, into my very being, as my eyes go wide, almost as if someone has dumped ice-cold water over me. My eyes lock onto his as the lack of oxygen sends black spots dancing through my vision. But still I see him crystal clear through the haze.

His usual shaggy blonde hair is slicked back, and his brown eyes, which used to remind me of chocolate, now look like they are glowing red. His lips, the same lips that I wanted to kiss only moments ago, now seem like death as they curl up into a devious grin. I feel like I have just been punched in the gut as my stomach twists harshly into knots. I start feeling faint, almost as if I'm going to pass out. Then, suddenly to my surprise the pressure on my throat eases. Oxygen comes rushing past my lips as I greedily suck in the air.

"Please!" I plead, my voice sounding raspy from being choked. "Don't do this!" He chuckles as if I just told a joke. Grabbing me by the elbow, he forcibly pulls me back to his car.

I start screaming and trying to pull away; he covers my mouth with his hand, and his arm wraps my waist as we continue toward the car. Biting down, I feel his skin between my teeth for a split second as I bring my elbow back, hitting him in the stomach. I get the sweet release that I was hoping for and sprint forward. But I don't make it more than a couple of steps. When I feel his grip again, taking hold of my elbow. Spinning me to face him, I watch in horror as he raises his hand. Before I can defend myself, his hand comes speeding toward me.

Violet S.R. Cox

There's a blinding pain as his palm meets my cheek with enough force to send me falling to the ground on all fours, the tiny pieces of gravel biting into the soft flesh of my palms and knees. The taste of copper fills my mouth as tears blur my vision. He wraps his hand into my long hair, roughly dragging me to my feet. Strands of hair rip out of my scalp as I struggle to stand. The pain vibrates through my head. When I finally get up, he roughly pulls my hair down behind my back, forcing me to meet his cruel cold gaze.

"I always get what I want. Now stop being a bitch," he growls at me; I can tell he's losing his patience. He drags me back to his car by my hair as I scream and plead for mercy. I try to dig my feet into the hard, unforgiving ground, but with no luck. *Who was I to think that I could escape from the quarterback?* I wonder to myself. I feel the fight in me start to distinguish as I grow tired.

He finally gets me back to his car, opens the back driver-side door, and shoves me onto the black leather seat. Rolling onto my stomach, I try to dash for the passenger door. But he is faster. He grabs my ankles and drags me back toward him. Rolling me over onto my back, his hands go to the front of my dress. The horrible sound of torn fabric fills the empty air of the car as he rips my beautiful dress to the hem. I desperately try to push his hands away, but to no avail. I pound my fist against his chest, trying anything I can do to escape.

Grabbing my hands, he pins them above my head. I once again feel the sense of dread that flooded me only minutes ago as I realize that I have lost.

I am about to be raped.

My stomach twists into knots, and wet, warm tears streak down my cheeks as his free hand goes to my panties, tugging on them. *No, no, please, no,* I silently pray to myself. Getting aggravated, he lets go of my hands. *This is my chance.* I think to myself as I reach desperately for the door handle above my

Sweet Vengeance

head; as I try to kick him, he rips my underwear off me. He catches my leg and pushes himself between my thighs as he pins my hands once more above my head.

I try everything I can think of to get out from under him. But he is much stronger than I am and weighs more than my fragile and petite body. Glancing up at him, I see him creepily admiring my mostly exposed body as if I were a piece of meat to be devoured.

"I think we can get rid of this god-awful bra," he says out loud, smiling as if he has just won the lottery. His free hand reaches for the clasp on the front of my bra, unclipping it; he moves it to either side of me, exposing my breast.

"Oh my… you are breathtaking. Better than I could have ever imagined," he breathes, admiring my naked body. Reaching out, he strokes my breast. His touch trails down my body, reminding me of the touch of death as it leaves behind chills.

Pulling his hand from my body, I desperately hope he is starting to feel guilty and will let me go. *Please have mercy. Please have a heart.* The thoughts vanish as quickly as they came, when I hear the slight jingle of him undoing his belt, followed by the sound of him unzipping his pants. I clench my eyes shut, tears silently falling down my cheeks. Something hard and warm presses against me down below.

"I told you I always get what I want," he states coldly, his voice void of any emotion. "Now, darling, why don't you be a good girl and take me."

He rubs my most intimate spot before grabbing his member and forcibly shoving himself into my entrance. The tearing pain rips through my body as if I am being stretched to the point of being split in half. *This was not how my first time was supposed to be,* I think to myself.

Violet S.R. Cox

I turn my face away, burying it into my arm, trying to envision anything, *anything* at all to flood out the assault. It's funny what the brain comes up with to drown out an terrifying event. *I really should have pushed myself harder. I should have built up my stamina. But I was always in too much pain to run due to the daily abuse.*

Time seems to stop as I lose myself in my own thoughts and memories.

I am staring out my bedroom window, watching the sky turn orange as the sun slowly descends behind the trees. Watching the sunset was always so calming and beautiful. The pinkish-orange glow kissing the earth goodnight.

His free hand grabs my hip, his callused fingertips bite into my skin roughly, tearing me from the welcomed distraction. The sounds of his moans of pleasure fill the silent car, making me nauseous. After what feels like an eternity, he lets out a loud moan as he thrusts deeply one last time, nearly collapsing on top of me breathless.

"God, you were amazing," he says as he tries to catch his breath—as if what he had just done was consensual. To my relief, he pulls himself out of me as he buttons up his pants. I curl up on my side in a fetal position, trying to cover my naked body with my ragged clothes. My face is soaked from all the tears I shed during the assault. My whole body aches in places I never thought possible.

"Oh, don't be like that, Scarlett. You enjoyed every minute of it, and you know it," he tells me. I watch him admire what he can of my bare skin before he suddenly grabs my feet.

I urgently claw for the edge of the seat as he drags me out of the car. I feel the leather seat sliding under me, followed by a brief nothingness before the brutal impact of my head hitting the door jam sends a blinding wave of pain through my skull. Stars dance in my vision, and the sudden impact of my body hitting the ground knocks the breath out of me. I try to open my eyes as I fade in and out of the darkness. The dirt road slides beneath me rough like sandpaper biting into my skin as I am dragged across the ground. I open my eyes briefly to see that he's pulled me to the side of the road.

I catch a glance of him as he brings his foot back. It collides against my rib cage, and I hear the *crack* of one of my ribs being broken from the force as a fresh wave of pain floods my body. Rolling over onto my side, I curl up in a ball trying to shield myself, as he starts kicking me in the stomach and the back of my head.

The nightmare fades as my eyes snap open.

CHAPTER 2

    I jolt awake, shaking, drenched in a cold sweat. My eyes dart around the empty room, searching frantically for any lurking figures that don't belong as the sound of my pulsating heart floods my ears. My gaze passes over the dark shadows of furniture. The room is empty, just as I left it before I fell asleep only a few hours ago. I suddenly realize the satin sheets are tangled around my legs from tossing and turning

    Thank god, it was just a nightmare. I think, taking a shaky breath, trying to calm my anxiety and exhaling slowly as my body trembles. *I can't believe that even after two years, I still get nightmares that leave me filled with dread.* Dropping my head into my hands, I fight the urge to just let the tears flow. My tangled dark hair falls forward; creating a curtain of darkness around my face as I battle my own personal demons threating to overtake me. I have grown accustomed to having panic attacks.

    A yelp sounds from my lips, at the sudden knocking on my door echoing through the silent room, causing me to jump. My eyes snap to my bedroom door as it slowly creaks open, revealing a six-foot silhouette. I already know who it is as he cautiously walks to my bed. In the darkness, I can tell that his jet-black hair is loose from its everyday ponytail. I feel his ice-blue eyes weighing on me as he studies me. His concern radiates in almost unbearable waves.

"Selen, honey, are you okay?" Jay asks as he sits on the edge of the bed, watching me closely. His calm, reassuring voice reminds me of a caring father worried about his little girl. I had never seen so much kindness or love until I met him. Unlike my biological father, Jay always treated me like I was his flesh and blood. He has always been there when I needed him, whether it is teaching me to fight or ensuring I was safe.

I wish my parents showed this much concern or cared about my well-being.

"It was just a nightmare, sweetie," he adds, trying to comfort me like he has so many times before.

"No, it was real," I mutter, almost in tears, as the memories of that horrible night flood my brain. The fear-filled night of my rape fresh in my mind—the night that I died and was given a new life.

Two years ago, I awoke to excruciating pain flooding every inch of my body. I could feel it in my toes and even my fingertips as I curl in on myself, trying to ease the unimaginable agony. At this point, I pull at the torn dress that is now nothing but a rag to cover my exposed body the best I can. The spring air gradually getting colder with every passing minute. It hurts to breathe, each inhale of air causes a sharp, dagger-like pain in my ribs.

Violet S.R. Cox

Maybe I wouldn't be alone in the dark on an abandoned road if I gave Abe what he wanted. Maybe if I just gave in, he wouldn't have left me. There were so many "maybes" as I started blaming myself.

I stare at the looming dark trees that remind me of arms reaching out as if to snatch me up. The sound of crickets chirping and frogs croaking fills the dark night air. I lay there listening to the sounds of nature surrounding me as I fade in and out from the pain racking my body.

I didn't know how long I had been there when the sound of a vehicle approaching brought me to. The headlights blinding me as they approach, and I shield my eyes against the bright light as a figure climbs out of the car. I begin to shake uncontrollably, thinking Abe has returned. Fear fills my body, awakening the breathtaking pain that rattles me like an earthquake. I watch in horror as the figure runs to my side.

Why can't he just let me die in peace? Hasn't he tortured me enough? What if he didn't get enough and returned to rape me again? Questions about the worst possible scenarios flood my mind.

The figure comes to a kneeling halt beside me, blocking some of the glow from the headlights. Casting me in a dark shadow, I glance up at the figure, partially relieved to realize that the body build doesn't match Abe's.

"Miss, oh my God. What happened?" he asks me as shock fills his voice. I can't see any of his features with the headlights shining from behind him, but it seems like his hair is black. The tears start falling again for what feels like the thousandth time tonight.

"Who are you?" I weakly ask as I start to feel numb. "Did he send you to kill me?"

Sweet Vengeance

He studies me, confused. His eyes scan my form, taking in my bruised and battered body. He reaches for me, causing me to jerk away, terrified. Pain shoots through my body like a tsunami; I grit my teeth together as I suppress a scream that wants to escape my lips. Immediately, he withdraws his hands and holds both up in a peaceful gesture.

"It's okay. It's okay. I am not here to hurt you, miss. I live down the road," he explains, pointing in the opposite direction. "I saw you out here and stopped. My name is Jay Samuels." He reaches into his jean pocket, pulling out a cell phone. "I'm going to call for help," he adds as he dials a number.

"Don't," I tell him. "There is no point."

He glances down at me, confused. "Why not?" he asks me, looking me over again. "You need help."

"They won't make it in time," I start to explain as I gag, coughing up blood. "I am pretty sure I am bleeding internally. Plus, I deserve this." I start to feel very lightheaded. Even from my place on the ground, I feel like I'm about to fall.

"No one deserves this," he tells me, sounding sincere. He reaches for me again but stops, his hands hanging midair. He must have seen the fear in my eyes. "I am going to help you sit up," he calmly explains, trying to reassure me as he does so. Every little move triggers waves of pain, making me cry out. Apologizing, he kneels next to me to help me sit upright, letting me use him as support.

The pain is beginning to fade. I can feel my body losing the fight as I cough up more blood into my hands. The warm liquid floods my palms like I scooped up a handful of water. I glance over at him to find him staring at my hands, his eyes wide with shock. I could see that he was thinking of a way to help me. With the light on his face illuminating his features, kindness radiates from deep within his ice-blue eyes. His skin, kissed by the sun, is lightly tanned. His hair is black as the night sky, pulled back into a short ponytail.

"I think you are right about bleeding internally," he tells me, breaking the silence. "Without help, you will die," he adds as if trying to change my mind about getting help. The mention of dying should scare me, but I'm strangely calm.

"I know. It is what it is." I reply numbly, my voice void of any emotion.

"Would you at least like me to call your parents for you? I know they have to be worried sick," he says with obvious concern.

"They would jump with joy."

"Why do you say that?"

"They abuse me on a regular basis," I say in a careless tone, shrugging. "So they'll be glad to be rid of me… I have accepted the fact that my parents didn't love me a long time ago. I was just trying to make it to my eighteenth birthday so I could legally leave."

He goes silent as he processes that information, almost as if he is determining if I am telling the truth, before taking a deep breath. He looks around us before turning his gaze back to me.

"I can give you a second chance and a better life," he tells me, sounding confident.

I look at him in confusion. *How could he give me a second chance at life? What could he possibly mean? Was he delusional?*

Sweet Vengeance

"How?" I ask as black spots weave into my vision. My voice sounds muffled to my own ears. I feel the coldness overtaking my body, and the pain has vanished. My head is fuzzy, almost like I am lost in a mist.

Death isn't too far away now, patiently waiting for me to succumb. I know I should be terrified, but here I am, about to die, and I couldn't care less. I am just *numb*. It wasn't like anyone would notice or care if I lived or died.

"I have this special ability to heal people depending on how badly they are injured," he says. "With how bad your injuries are, it would change—"

"What do you mean that you can heal people?" I ask, confused as the darkness slowly dances around the edge of my vision, almost as if waiting to swallow me whole.

"I am immortal. I can turn you whi—"

"Immortals are fictional." I interrupt, thinking he is just pulling my leg. He studies me as he tries to figure out how to make me believe. He reaches out his hand and places it over a black and blue bruise on my arm. A bright golden light floods from his hand and slowly seeps into my flesh. *What the?* My foggy, tired brain cannot comprehend what I'm witnessing as the dark black and blue bruise slowly fade until it is completely gone within seconds. My eyes go wide in shock as the bruise is replaced with my usual paleness. Meeting his eyes in bewilderment, I ask. "How did you do that?" In disbelief, I stare back at my arm as if the bruise will reappear. As if it was just covered up with makeup.

"As I said, I am an immortal. I could give you a second chance if you want it," he says softly. My eyelids were heavy as lead, and I felt them closing for the last time. With how severe my injuries were, no one could save me, not even an immortal with healing abilities. I was nothing but a waste of space anyways. No one would miss me, so why not just give into the darkness waiting to accept me? But something deep within me wants to live, but only for one reason and that reason alone.

"I would love another chance at life so I can get revenge, but my injuries are too severe for anyone to repair," I tell him as the darkness latches onto me, pulling me into its depths. I fade into the blackness, welcoming it as it swallows me, but not before I hear him say one last thing:

"You just wait and see. You will have your second chance."

I fade utterly into the waiting darkness, my life slowly slipping away piece by piece as death embraces me.

I feel like I'm floating on a cloud as I slowly blink my eyes open against a bright white light. The cold, hard ground is no longer beneath me, and the pain is entirely gone, replaced by warmth. The calmness and silence is so peaceful—this must be Heaven.

My eyes finally adjust to the bright light. I glance around, trying to figure out where I am. But I don't recognize my surroundings: a living room that I had never been in before. I am lying on a gray couch with a blue blanket over me; two matching recliners on the other side of the room. I slowly sit up as I take it all in, the confusion of not knowing where I am growing more profound.

Where am I? And how did I get here? I start questioning as I look around uneasily. *What happened? At least the nightmare isn't absolute, or was it?*

I hear the sound of soft footsteps approaching from behind me, causing me to jolt off the couch and see whom the footsteps belong to. I look into the man's face only to realize it is the same one from my dream. He is dressed in black sweats and a white t-shirt. His name was Jay, or at least it was in my nightmare.

He keeps his distance as he walks around the couch and sits in one of the gray recliners. That is when I realize that I'm only wearing a baggy t-shirt that ends at my mid-thigh. I slowly glance down at my skin to find it caked with dirt. The realization of what I thought was only a nightmare actually happened slams into me, almost knocking the breath out of me and suffocating me as reality sinks in. The world crashes down around me as I fight to breathe. All I can do is stare at the guy who saved me.

"Take deep breaths. You are having a panic attack," he instructs me calmly as he stands up and walks toward me, causing me to quickly step away. He freezes and makes calming gestures with his hand.

"Deep breath in."

I take a deep breath in.

"Now, slowly, exhale."

Once again, I do as instructed. After a few times, my breathing returns back to normal, and my pounding heart begins to slow.

"I never have panic attacks," I say quietly.

"With trauma, it is normal," he explains. He gestures to the couch as he sits back down in the recliner.

I return to my spot on the couch and look around the living room. It's quite basic with its simple furniture and television. The walls are a beautiful bright shade of gray, like rain clouds gathering in the sky; the black and white tiles remind me of a checkerboard.

An awkward silence falls between us.

"How are you feeling?" he asks, breaking the silence and staring at me with concern filling his eyes. I swallow past the lump in my throat, trying to find my voice.

"I feel alright," I answer numbly. *But I don't understand how I am alive.*

"I think you know the answer."

When he answers my unspoken thought, I look at him with bewilderment.

"Did you just….. Did you just read my mind?" I ask. He doesn't say anything as his eyes meet mine.

"Yes. I told you I would give you a second chance at life, Selen." His voice fills my head, which causes me to jump. I stare at him in disbelief as I realize what he says is true.

Well, I will be damned. *Immortals actually do exist*, and one has granted me a second chance at life. It all sounds too bizarre to be authentic. But when I should be dead, I'm alive and breathing.

I glance up at him as I slowly realize that I really did die. This man sitting before me brought me back to life.

"So I am immortal now; what exactly does that mean?" I curiously ask as I start to remember everything more clearly. I feel the anger burning deep within me. It begins to overtake me. My whole body is on fire, my blood is boiling, and the need for revenge runs deep in my veins. That bastard will pay for what he did. One way or another I will exact my revenge against the guilty party.

"Selen, sweetheart, are you okay?" The sound of Jay's voice pulls me back to the present moment.

I look up at the present Jay compared to the Jay from the past. It took him months to earn my trust. He didn't just give me another chance; he also helped me adapt to my new life as an immortal, and to deal with the nightmares that still haunt my dreams on a regular basis. He has become more like a father to me. More of a father than my own dad ever was. I have never known someone so caring until I met him. I owe him everything.

But that was a debt that I would never be able to fulfill.

"I just wish these nightmares would go away," I mutter, feeling defeated.

"I know," he says gingerly, "and in time, they will. You just have to be patient. What you went through was traumatic. But for now I want you to try to get some more sleep before our training session today."

He stands up from the bed, leans over, and kisses my forehead like a father would with his daughter. I nod in agreement, knowing I need more sleep than two to three hours a night. I curl up beneath the covers feeling like a little girl who had her dad check under her bed for monsters. His footsteps echo down the stairs as he leaves to return to his house, which isn't far from mine. The door closes softly as he exits before I fade into the peacefulness of sleep.

CHAPTER 3

After awaking the following morning, I get dressed in my workout clothes: a red tank top and camouflage workout pants. My long dark hair is tied back into a ponytail. I find myself standing at the edge of an old training field behind our houses, roughly cut into the dense strands of pine and oak trees. It reminds me of the course you would see on the Marine bases because it had similar obstacles like the wall climb, rope climb, and monkey bars. This course was meant to build upper strength.

To the left side of the obstacle course hangs a heavy punching bag, and to the right lays the sparring mats. A man-made structure provides cover overhead. On the only wall of the structure are targets made out of plywood designed for throwing knives, which Jay would occasionally use them for archery.

Walking into the center of the sparring mat, I start by stretching, trying to warm up my muscles while I wait patiently for Jay to arrive. I am early today, unlike every other day. I move my head from side to side, then do a head roll to loosen up my neck muscles. I roll my shoulders back and forth, then stretch my arms across my body. I feel myself loosening up. Positioning myself forward, I start doing some push-ups, warming up my muscles before going to the course.

Sweet Vengeance

I walk over to the wall climbing course and study it. It's basically a bunch of decking boards nailed flush against each other to two posts on either side. The top of the wall stands eight feet off the ground.

I take a deep breath before sprinting toward it, knowing that a running start is the key to getting over it. I plant one foot on the wall as the other propels me to the top. My hands grab the edge, and I pull myself up and over, landing with a soft thud on the other side.

A smile spreads across my face, from feeling successful as I recall the first few times I tried this course. I failed miserably back then. I don't know how often I ran into the wall at full speed due to the fact I was uncoordinated. Take it from my personal experience, that kissing the wall like that really doesn't feel good. As a matter of fact, it hurts like hell. Even after figuring out the trick to getting over the wall, I always managed to find a new painful way of landing, whether it be falling on my ass, flat on my back, or even landing on my feet but spraining my knee or ankle in the process.

I sprint to the next obstacle: the monkey bars. Which stands about fifteen feet off the ground and are twenty feet long. I climb the ladder leading up to the first bar, grab it, and swing to the next. I glance at the sand below me. I swear I can see every imprint of the falls I took when I first started training.

It wasn't the fall that hurt; the sudden stop at the end did me in every time. I would land on my back or face-plant, resulting in a mouth full of gritty, disgusting sand. Trust me when I say that doing a belly buster on sand doesn't feel good.

I make it to the last bar. As I climb down the ladder, I can feel my arms starting to burn from the workout.

Violet S.R. Cox

After planting my feet safely back on the ground, I head toward the rope climb—the last course. Two large poles used for docks stand twenty-five feet in the air, supporting a large slab of wood across them. Two ropes hang from the slab of wood. This is the tough one, not that the rest were a walk in the park.

I chuckle remembering the painful falls I took off these ropes. I would make it about a quarter of the way up before falling painfully on my ass like Mulan did when they were trying to climb the pole. Come to think of it, most of my first few months of training were just like Mulan's training.

Shaking the memories away, I clear my head and take one of the ropes in my hand. I pull myself up and propel my body with my feet, bracing the rope. I am about halfway up, concentrating on just myself and the rope.

"Selen, would you hurry up and get down here already!"

Jay's voice booms loudly in my head, startles me causing me to lose concentration. I lose my grip on the rope.

Ah, Shit. I think as I brace for the hard impact I know is to follow. I land flat on my back, knocking the breath out of my lungs. I lay there struggling to breathe momentarily, staring up at the sunny baby-blue sky.

Jay walks over to where I am lying, shaking his head. "I did not tell you to fall," he sarcastically tells me, with smirk painted on his face.

"But you did tell me to hurry up and get down," I say, pausing to take a deep painful breath. "So, I decided to take the easy way down," I add sarcastically.

Jay rolls his eyes extending his hand out to me, which I gratefully accept. He pulls me up, and I dust the sand off of myself.

Sweet Vengeance

"You do realize that you are an ass sometimes, right?" I state. Causing him to arch an eyebrow in amusement.

"You have to learn not to be startled so easily," he retorts, chuckling before walking away from me and toward the sparring mats.

I follow him, hating the fact that he's right. He walks over to a duffle bag that he always brings with him. Reaching into the duffle, he pulls out identical blades. He hands them to me, and I take them carefully.

"I got these for you," he explains as I admire the six-inch daggers. The black handles have a purple gem inlaid in them and fits perfectly into the palms of my hands. The sun reflects off the sharp stainless steel blades nearly blinding me. I toss the one in my right hand, getting a feel for it.

"How do they feel?" he asks, studying me.

Reaching back into the duffle, he pulls out a set of throwing knives with purple handles and black blades, along with a two-inch that can be concealed.

"These are also for you," he states handing them to me.

Setting the larger daggers down on a small nearby table. I gingerly accept the weapons from him. Removing one of the throwing blades from the sheath, I balance it on my finger, checking the balance. Grabbing the hilt, I walk over toward the targets flipping it in the air. Weighing it in my hand like he taught me to do. Grabbing it by the blade, I fling it at the target. I watch as the blade spins slicing through the air. Until it hits almost dead center, echoed by a soft thud of the blade meeting wood. I smile, looking over at Jay.

"I love them," I tell him as I walk to the target, yanking the blade out and slipping it back into its sheath.

"I figured it was time for you to have your own set," he tells me, smiling. "Now, why don't we get some training in?" he says, returning to mentor mode as his voice turns serious, almost sounding like a drill sergeant. I nod in agreement.

"What are we working on today?" I ask curiously as we step onto the mats.

"Today's lesson is attacking," he explains in the same powerful mentor voice he always uses during these sessions. "You will fight as hard as you can against me. Don't worry, you won't hurt me. So, *No* holding back." He stands there staring at me waiting. Looking almost careless.

With no response, I dig my foot into the ground, pushing myself into a sprint toward him. Swinging as hard as I can when I reach him. He sidesteps at the last minute, my hands not even coming close as he completely evades me. I stumble and nearly fall, but he grabs me by the wrist to steady me. Using this chance I launch myself at him, but he grabs my fist mid-swing. I kick my foot this time, determined to land at least one hit. Dropping my hand, he blocks my leg. I try to use this distraction and try for a punch, but he blocks me with his arm with minimal effort.

"You aren't even trying," he barks at me.

Which infuriates me, sparking a new determination. Striking with my hand first, distracting him as I slip my leg behind his. He blocks my fist and I pull my leg back quickly. His eyes go wide as he falls backward with a soft thud. Staring up at me in surprise.

Sweet Vengeance

"Not bad," he compliments, pushing himself off the ground.

A twig snaps behind me snagging my attention. I feel a brief moment of air as he trips me. Landing on my back I glare up at him as I lay there.

"Always expect the unexpected, and don't get distracted," he lectures sternly.

Extending his hand out to me. I lean up, reaching for it, before snaking my legs around his and throwing my body to the side. His legs go from under him and he falls to the mats with a quiet thud. He looks over at me from the ground.

"That wasn't fair," he complains.

I smile triumphantly at him. "Expect the unexpected. You just preached it to me," I tell him, being a smart ass once more.

"Good, so you did learn," he comments as he pushes himself off the ground, gesturing for me to do the same.

He readies himself before sprinting at me, switching tactics. Making me go on the defense. When he is in reach, I swing, but he steps back. While I am off balance, he grabs my outstretched arm and drops suddenly, facing the other way. Which sends me flying over his shoulder. I land hard on the mats back first and lay there motionless, trying to regain my breathing.

"I think that is enough for the day," he tells me as he ends the training session.

"No, I can still fight. I just need a moment," I insist.

"I know you can, but I don't want you overworking yourself," he says, shaking his head as he sits on the mat. His mentor voice replaced with a caring tone.

"Fine." I don't move; I lie there letting my breathing returns to normal.

"So, what do I need to work on?" I ask him, staring at the metal on the roof. After all, this is the part where we usually discuss what I am lacking.

"Actually, nothing. You are thinking quicker on the spot," he says. "That has always been your main problem. You take too long to plan and overthink things."

I glance over at him, surprised. "What exactly does that mean?" I ask, confused. "Do I need to train more?"

"No, I am saying I think you are ready. You have all the training you need," he explains, which stuns me.

"No, no. I think I need more training," I mumble as doubt seeps into me, afraid I might screw up.

"You got this. Just remember your training, and you will be fine," he reassures me. "You have to spread your wings in order to fly."

Knowing he is right, I nod in agreement standing up. I feel a new found hope flood me. He wouldn't say I was ready if I wasn't. He has always been honest with me.

Tonight, my mission is strictly to gather intel on my rapist.

Sweet Vengeance

Pulling my hair back, I place the blond wig on my head, adjusting it in the mirror. It's funny how just a simple hair color can change your appearance. My usual pale skin now looks tan. My green eyes look brighter under the bangs of the wig. Putting on the final touches, I glance in the mirror to find a young woman looking back at me that I don't recognize.

Walking out my door toward the thinly wooded area that separates us, I go to Jay's house to borrow his truck.

CHAPTER 4

    This local bar has definitely seen better days. The dim lighting almost hides how the white paint on the walls is starting to chip, revealing the previous red beneath, like specks of random blood against the tacky white. The black-painted floor is faded; you can see the gray of concrete trying to peek through from the highly traveled path. The neon bar signs and pool table lamp are the only light provided, shining through the small dark bar. The local customers crowding the bar are almost three sheets to the wind, nearly overpowering the music.

    I'm sitting at one of the tables furthest away from the bar, tucked in a dark corner, sipping on a pineapple and Malibu mixed drink. I watch as my rapist downs another shot, then staggers toward a blonde woman sitting at the end of the bar. She is wearing a black miniskirt and a strapless red top. She runs her hand down his chest seductively; and he starts groping her.

    His hands travel my skin, leaving behind trails of coldness in their wake. My heart races in my chest as fear slams into my body, knowing that I have lost as the tears stream down my cheeks.

Sweet Vengeance

Tearing my eyes away from them, I gaze toward the pool table as I try to push the unwelcome dark memories away. *Take a deep breath, Selen. Calm down,* I tell myself as I try to battle the anxiety attack that wants to overwhelm me.

Tonight, I needed to focus.

At the pool table, I watch as two guys walk up—most likely brothers, considering they share similar features: hazel eyes and the same dirty blonde hair. One was cleaned and shaved, while the other had a stubbly beard, looking like he was trying to grow it out. If I had to guess their age difference, I'd assume there was at least a two-year gap by how they teased each other.

The one I assume is older pockets the eight ball, leaving one lonely ball on the table.

"That was luck," the other one says as they walk away from the pool table.

Sore from sitting for so long, I get up and decide to try my luck. I walk to the side of the table, putting the dollar worth of quarters into the slot, pushing the small silver lever in, and pulling it back out. I hear the clank of the pool balls rolling as they drop into the ball return.

"Would you mind if I shoot a game with you?" I hear a man's voice say from behind me. It startles me a little, but not nearly as bad as usual.

Be calm. Act normal.

I turn toward the voice, not imagining I'll find a guy with black hair shaved on the sides and back, long on the top of his head, braided. It reminds me of a Viking hairstyle, which I believe he was going for, and it suits him. His eyes are a grayish blue like storm clouds threatening the pale sky.

"Yeah, sure. I don't know if I'm any good, though," I answer him. "My name is Claire." The lie comes easily.

"I'm Alarik," he introduces himself as he walks toward the drop box, grabbing the balls and putting them in the raggedy wooden rack. "Don't worry, I'm not any good either," he says as he pushes the rack to the dot.

Grabbing a cue stick from the rack bolted to the wall, I glance at the bar to find Abe still groping the blonde as he sips his beer occasionally. You can tell he is intoxicated by the way he is swaying and staggering.

Trying to push down the fear telling me to run, I take a deep breath to calm down as I turn away from the bar and toward the pool table. Alarik slowly pulls the rack away before moving off to the side, leaving a nice triangle of colorful balls at the end of the table. He hands the dingy white ball toward me.

I place the cue ball behind the header before leveling myself with the table. I grasp the rail, with the tip of the cue stick between my ring finger and middle finger, holding just tight enough to move it. My right hand is about halfway up the base of the stick. I move my right arm back and forth, striking the white cue ball, sending it into the front ball. The pool table is littered with color as the balls scatter each and every way. Standing up, I watch the solid purple ball fall into the far corner pocket.

"Solids," Alarik says. "That was a good break."

Sweet Vengeance

"Thank you," I reply as I study the table, looking for a shot. I go with the burgundy ball sitting off to the side of the center pocket. I level myself with the table and hit the cue ball, trying to cut it into the pocket. But it hits the side rail.

I stand and back away from the table as Alarik studies it. Glancing at the bar and to see Abe handing a shot to the blonde as he downs his. *Maybe if I can get her drunk enough, she'll let me fuck her.* His inner thoughts flood my head, clearly sending shivers down my spine.

Taking a deep breath, I mentally push his thoughts away, as Jay has taught me. His voice is getting loud, and his words are starting to slur together from the effects of the liquor he has been inhaling for the past hour.

Glancing back at the pool table, I watch as Alarik levels himself with the table. His eyes study a green striped ball on the rail about a foot from the corner pocket. He does a few practice strokes before gently tapping the cue ball into the striped ball, which rolls down the rail and into the pocket.

"Nice shot," I comment as he stands and walks around the table. He levels himself with the table once more.

"Thanks," he replies with a small smirk of satisfaction. I notice he glances up from his object ball to the bar before returning his eyes to the table.

He hits the cue ball into his target ball, but it bounces off the rail, going toward the opposite side of the table. He steps away as I step up, studying my choices.

Settling on the yellow ball, I turn, exposing my back to the bar. A few short moments later I hear a loud crash, followed by yelling behind me. I spin around to find a fight breaking out and heading my way. Someone tugs me out of the way as two guys fall onto the pool table, sending the pool balls scattering across the surface.

And to no surprise, one of them is Abe.

"Are you okay?" I hear Alarik's voice from beside me as we watch a bunch of people run toward the fight trying to pull them apart.

"Yeah, thank you," I tell him. As we move away from the fight, I add, "Well, it looks like our game is over."

The onlookers finally break up the two men; Abe storms out of the bar, muttering angrily with blood trailing from his nose. He glances at me as he walks past, causing me to inwardly cringe, holding my breath, hoping he won't recognize me. I don't see any spark of recognition as he walks out the door.

Exhaling, I glance at the clock in the bar, pretending to be checking the time. "It was nice meeting you and it was a nice game while it lasted, but unfortunately, I have to go," I lie once more.

"Yeah, stupid drunks," he says, rolling his eyes. "Be safe," he adds as he walks toward the back of the bar.

As soon as I open the door and step outside, the hot summer air almost takes my breath away as it wraps around my body like a second skin. I watch Abe stumble into his blue Ford pickup as I walk to Jay's truck, where I've carefully backed into a dark spot behind Abe's vehicle.

I slide onto the cloth seats and watch as Abe leans out of his truck, puking. *Dumb-ass, that's what you get,* I think to myself. When he's finally done vomiting, he closes his truck door, and I hear the engine rattle to life as he starts it.

Sweet Vengeance

He pulls out of the parking spot, and I pull out after him, careful to stay a little ways back.

After a few minutes of following his truck in the dark, he pulls into a driveway before a red brick house, with black shutters on either side of the windows. I park off to the side of the road a few houses down. I watch him stumble out of the truck and up to the dark brick house. I carefully check my surroundings before stepping out of the truck and silently approaching the home.

I walk around the side of the house, looking for any open blinds to get an idea of what the inside looks like. Finally, I find a window with light shining out and carefully look in to find a messy room. Clothes are scattered all over the floor, including the bed on which he is lying face down, looking like he passed out. I quietly back away from the window.

Walking around the corner to return to the truck, I slam into something solid and fall backward, landing painfully on my ass. I look up, unsure of what I just ran into, to find Alarik's gaze on me as he catches a blade he was tossing in the air.

What the?

"Claire?" he questions, confused.

"Uh, yeah. Um, hi," I reply awkwardly as I quickly stand up, dusting the dirt off me. "What are you doing here?" I question as I watch the blade in his hand.

Why does he have a knife?

"I could ask you the same thing," he states coldly, studying me intently. "How do you know Abe?"

"Um, well, I am his ex," I say— at least it's the partial truth.

"So you decided to stalk your ex?" he asks, raising his eyebrows. "Never mind, it doesn't matter. You need to leave. I don't want you becoming a complication," he says, his voice taking on a cold tone.

"Complication? What exactly are you planning?" I ask, crossing my arms over my chest.

"You seem nice if not a bit naive, but I don't want to hurt you. So leave. Now!" he instructs before stepping around me like I was a child being dismissed.

I am surprised when a soft laugh escapes my mouth. "You couldn't hurt me, even if you tried," I say, turning around to look at him.

Alarik stops dead in his tracks and glares back at me; if looks could kill, I would be dead.

"Fuck it," he growls, turning to face me. "Don't say I didn't warn you."

He throws his blade. I watch it come hurling toward me, and I duck at the last second, feeling the rush of air as it glides over my head. I hear the soft thud of it hitting a tree a few feet behind me. I stand up, to find Alarik gaping at me in shock before he switches back to his cold stare and approaches me.

"Don't say I didn't warn you when you end up on your ass," I tell him, smiling, which irritates him more.

He walks up and swings his fist toward me, which I block easily. *So you want to play?* I think to myself as I bring my fist forward and into his chest, making him stumble back, which stuns him for a split second. He lets out a soft growl of annoyance. He runs at me, and I sidestep and kick my leg out, tripping him and send him to the ground. Instead of face-planting like most would do, he goes shoulder-first into the ground and rolls back up to a standing position. He lands just in front of the tree, pulling the blade from the trunk before throwing it at me again. It flies past me; I watch it bounce off the brick house with a loud clanking noise.

The next thing I know, I am on the ground, staring up at Alarik. He's standing over me, breathing heavily, holding another knife to my throat. My own breathing comes in hard gasps as I glare up at him. *Damn it. You knew better,* I scold myself as I gaze up into his cold eyes.

"Now what?" he questions. Before I can answer, a light shines through the window closest to us. Grabbing his attention. *This is my chance.*

While he is distracted, I bring my arm up, hitting the knife out of his hand and kicking my legs under his, tripping him. I quickly scramble to my feet.

"That is what," I say lamely as he stares at me from the ground. We both see a shadow on the ground as it blocks the light from the window. Abe is awake, his shadow passing over us.

"Shit," we both say in unison.

Alarik pulls himself off the ground, grabbing the blade before darting into the dark night. I bolt in the opposite direction.

Once I'm back in the truck, I breathe a sigh of relief. I put it in drive and head home.

Violet S.R. Cox

By the time I pull into Jay's driveway, it's almost three in the morning. His house is dark; he must have gone to sleep. I climb out of the truck and take the short walk home. When I get through the door, I am totally exhausted.

I pull the blonde wig off my head, my dark hair falling from its cage as it slips past my shoulder. I lock the door behind me before heading up to my room. After unarming myself, I quickly shower to wash all the dirt and grime off before crawling into bed.

I can't stop thinking of Alarik. I recognize him from somewhere, but I can't place where.

Chapter 5

My forest green locker shuts with a loud metallic echo. The row of lockers and random posters were the only splash of color in the bare white hallway with the speckled black floor. The utter lack of color and strict uniform policy reminded me of prison, trapping me in the endless hallways and classes until two-thirty every day.

I head toward my second class, slamming into one of the football players, knocking all my books from my arms. I mumble an apology as I bend down to pick them up, my body protesting in pain. The football player mutters a rude comment before stepping around me.

A shadow passes over me, and I anticipate a teacher chastising me. To my surprise, the person kneels before me and helps me retrieve my books and stray sheets of paper. He stands and offers me his hand; I gratefully take it, getting to my feet. Looking up, I find a boy with slightly shaggy jet-black hair and stormy, piercing blue eyes.

"Thank you," I say, finding my voice; I never talked unless spoken to.

He gently takes the books from my hands, putting them on his stack.

"You don't have to do that," I say in a rush, not wanting to bother him any more than I already have.

Unexpectedly, he smiles at me in a shy, friendly way.

"You look like you are having a rough day," he says softly. "Plus, we also have English and math together. So what can it hurt?"

I guess I can't argue with that. I try to recall what his name is. What do his friends call him again?

"It's Rik, right?" I ask.

"Yeah," he replies as we weave through the crowd of students in the hallway. "It's short for Alarik. You're Scarlett, right?"

"Yeah, my parents have an amusing sense of humor," I tell him as we pass a cluster of students who don't care if they make it to their next class on time.

He glances over at me, studying me. "Taking a guess, you don't like the name Scarlett?" he asks, amused.

"No, I honestly hate it. I like my middle name better," I add as we round the corner toward room 122.

"Well, what's your middle name? If you don't mind me asking," he says as we pass more green lockers.

Sweet Vengeance

"Selen," I tell him. This is the most I have talked at all this year in school. It feels strange and comforting somehow.

"I think it fits you better, to be honest," he remarks as we come to our classroom door. He surprises me as he stops and gestures for me to enter first, with him following behind me through the rows of desks.

I walk to my desk, which is against the bright wall, and sit down in the hard green plastic seat that matches the lockers in the hall. He sets my books down on my desk gently.

"Thank you again," I say before he approaches the seat next to mine.

"No problem," he says as he pulls his notebook out.

I lean against the cold wall, stretching my legs. I pull out my sketchbook and pencils, which I always carry with me. I start drawing as the class begins to fill with students.

I awake to the sun shining through my window, lying there as I recall the dream. That would explain why I thought I recognized him. We went to school together, and he was the only kind person who actually took the time to help me. I recall Abe also teasing him and trying to torment him. Maybe that was why he was at Abe's house—trying to get revenge for all those times.

But why, after all these years?

Stretching, I drag myself out of the warm bed. Before leaving the house, I throw on a red tank top, a pair of black shorts, and dark sneakers. The South Carolina humidity is already making it warm but not unbearable, so I decide to walk instead of borrowing Jay's truck. I feel the sun's warmth kissing my skin as I walk into town.

    Walking on the sidewalk to the local coffee shop, I pass a few stores and tourists admiring the Town of Beaufort as they take pictures. I feel all the thoughts trying to invade my head, slamming down my mental wall I walk into the tiny coffee shop. The refreshing AC hits me in the face as I enter; I sigh as it caresses my skin.

    The cream walls, mahogany counter, and matching tables make it look like an upgraded version of the coffee shops you would see on television.

    Walking up to the counter to place my order, I feel the heavy weight of eyes on me. I glance around to find a familiar set of stormy blue eyes watching me from one of the tables, a coffee in front of him. He quickly glances away when he realizes I am looking at him. I turn my attention back to the short, stubby clerk behind the counter.

    "Morning," she greets me as I step up to the counter. Her fiery red hair is thrown up in a messy bun.

    "Morning," I greet back with a soft smile. "Can I get a small mocha iced coffee with extra cream and sugar, please?"

    She punches in the order, nodding as she calls out to her coworker while I slip her my cash. The coffee is ready by the time she hands me my change, which I put in the tip jar.

    "Thank you," I say before I sit at one of the tables, enjoying the AC a little longer. I feel the weight of eyes on me again.

Sweet Vengeance

Glancing up, I notice Alarik's gaze darting out the window he sits next to. *So he is watching.* For some odd reason, the thought of it gives me a glint of satisfaction.

After finishing my coffee and getting my share of the coolness the AC offers, I stand up and toss my plastic coffee cup away before walking out the door.

Onto the busy sidewalk, I sidestep to avoid running into a teen texting. I notice Alarik coming out of the coffee shop and turning toward me. Pretending not to see him, I walk into the crowd and brush past an older woman with her camera out, apologizing before I duck into one of the nearest stores.

Is he really following me? I think to myself as my nostrils are overwhelmed by dozens of scents. Looking around, I am surprised to find a bunch of candles and perfumes. *Since I am here, I might as well at least look around.*

I head to the fragrance section, pick two of my favorites, and pay for them. I can sense him in the store as I walk out. The soft thud of footsteps sounds behind me a few moments later, which reassures me that he is following me.

Rounding a corner that leads into an alley, I stop and lean against the wall, looking at the entrance with my arms across my chest to catch him off guard. He immediately comes to a halt when his eyes land on me.

"Why are you stalking me?" I demand curiously, hoping he hasn't realized I was Claire or remembered me from high school.

"How did you know I was following you?" he questions slowly turning red from the embarrassment of getting caught.

"It's kind of noticeable when you go everywhere I go," I say. "So again, I will ask. Why are you following me? That is a way to creep a girl out, you know."

"I...I thought I recognized you," he admits. "I was just trying to find out if you were who I thought you were without looking stupid. I'm sorry if that came off stalkerish," he adds, looking down at the ground.

Taking a deep breath, I push myself off the wall. "Hey, I have been there. But a bit of advice. Next time, you don't want to get noticed" I say. "Try to make it less obvious, like maybe walk on the other side of the street to keep an eye on them instead of being on their heels." My explanation earns me a weird look from Alarik.

"Well, thanks for the stalking advice, I guess," he replies awkwardly as he studies me, trying to figure me out.

Good luck, buddy.

"*If* you are gonna do it, at least do it right and don't get caught," I tell him before I walk past him. "Have a good day, sir."

I leave the alley and walk back onto the sidewalk, but not before I catch thoughts of his plans for the night in my head.

That was way too close, I think, taking a deep breath as I head back to my sanctuary.

Making it home, I decided to relax for the rest of the day. Once night falls, I get ready for tonight's adventure, putting on the blonde wig once more and ensuring I have my weapons before disappearing into the darkness.

Sweet Vengeance

This time, I think I can blend in better without the truck.

CHAPTER 6

Later that night, dressed in all black as Claire, I wait in the dark next to the bathroom, hoping my outfit will help me blend in. I watch a lone figure sitting in the dugout, waiting for someone, the moonlight casting the scene in its pale glow.

The sound of tires driving over gravel breaks the silence. I soon see the headlights as the truck parks in front of the baseball field across from me. The light from the cab shines onto the owner as he steps out of his vehicle.

He looked me in the eyes. "I always get what I want, Scarlett."

I catch my breath as I mentally push the flashback away. *No. I need to concentrate.* I watch Abe walk to the dugout, feeling a little queasy as my stomach tangles into knots. He's approaching the mystery guy that has been sitting there. When he closes the distance, he reaches into his pocket and pulls out something, handing it to the mystery man of the dark. In return, the mystery guy pushes something small into his hand, like a baggy of sorts.

Sweet Vengeance

Was this a drug deal? Since when does he do drugs?

Abe shoves the baggy into his pant pocket as he walks back to his vehicle, glancing around, almost as if nervous. Getting into his truck, he backs out and speeds away, gravel crunching beneath the tires as I watch the red glow of the brake lights vanish into the darkness.

Returning my attention to the drug dealer standing facing the road, I notice a silhouette drop gracefully to the ground out of a tree. The drug dealer spins, started by the soft thud of feet landing behind him. I don't even need to see his eyes to know they are stormy blue as I watch him slowly rise, his gaze trained on the drug dealer.

I silently but intently watch as the drug dealer steps away from Alarik, shocked, before regaining his composure. Alarik looks unbothered as he leans back against the tree, still focused on his target.

"I hear you are the person to see to get the good stuff," Alarik says, but it is faint; I can barely hear him from this spot. I lean forward, trying to stay tucked away in the shadows, straining to listen.

"Depends. What were you looking for?" the dealer asks as Alarik glances around the park before returning his cold stare to the drug dealer.

"Well, here's the problem," Alarik starts, "I'm not really here looking for drugs, but perhaps you could help me with something."

"What would that be?"

"Stop selling to that guy who just left," Alarik tells him with a hint of demand in his voice. I hear laughter flow to my ears as the drug dealer shakes his head in amusement.

"What makes you think that I would stop selling to my best customer just because some asshole playing Batman tells me to?" he asks.

Alarik stands straight, pushing away from the tree.

"I was kinda hoping you would say something along those lines," Alarik says just as he sprints toward the drug dealer. Before the guy can defend himself, I watch in horror as Rik wraps his hand around his throat. The dealer tries to break Alarik's hold, but he's soon lifted off the ground. I watch in utter silence and disbelief.

How is he so strong?

"Like I was saying, I really don't like that guy buying drugs from you," Alarik states. "He shouldn't be allowed to forget what he has done to innocents."

The drug dealer's eyes go wide from the lack of oxygen. Alarik releases his grip, causing him to fall to the ground roughly. I hear him coughing, trying to catch his breath as he reaches into his pocket, pulling out something; I know it's a blade by the way the moonlight reflects off the silver.

The drug dealer pulls himself off the ground. Alarik shakes his head and studies the guy in amusement.

His ego is going to get him killed if he isn't careful.

Sweet Vengeance

"I don't take demands," the dealer tells him as he holds the blade out before him.

Alarik looks away, shaking his head, almost as in disappointment, before his hand blurs as he grabs the dealer's arm, twisting and making him drop the blade that falls into the dirt.

"I usually don't ask twice due to the lack of patience," Alarik states, his voice cold.

I hear a loud snap as he twists the guy's arm; the dealer's pained scream fills the night air. Alarik lets go of him, and the dealer cradles his broken limb. I watch my old classmate bend down, picking something off the ground. I see a flash of light from his phone as he takes a picture of something before tossing whatever it was back at the dealer.

"I know where you live. So I suggest you take my advice and stop selling to Abe Smith. Or I will do worse than this," he tells him as he gestures toward the guy's arm. "Now leave before I change my mind."

The dealer nods before he takes off, running toward the parking lot. I watch as he hurriedly gets into a vehicle and speeds off to safety.

My eyes return to Alarik as he walks toward the playground beside me. He mutters something to himself as he passes the bathroom area.

"Well, that was nicely handled. If not a little brutal," I say from the darkness as I stand, causing him to halt and spin toward my voice. I step into the moonlight, revealing myself. The look of surprise is replaced by annoyance as he realizes who I am.

"Oh, yay. It's you again," he says sarcastically.

"Who were you expecting? The Easter Bunny?" I ask him as I cross my arms.

Growling in annoyance, he flings a blade toward me. It spins through the air, I duck, avoiding it easily.

What is with him and throwing knives? I think to myself as I stand back up.

I feel the sharp pain as the blade he holds bites into my shoulder, taking my breath away for a split second. Kicking him in the stomach, I send him stumbling backward. I wrap my hand around the blade that is buried up to its hilt in my flesh, taking a deep breath, I rip it out, causing more damage to the wound. I feel the warmth spread through the injury as my body mends the flesh together.

"Now, that wasn't very nice. Or fair," I tell him as I look back up at him, holding his blade in my hand.

Alarik stalks toward me, smiling, and I notice the silver of the moon reflecting from the stainless blade in his hand. I barely duck in time as his hand slashes above my head. Standing up when his hand passes over me, I grab his outstretched arm quickly, turning away from him and dropping to my knees. I propel him over me and onto the hard ground with a thud. I hear him try to regain his breathing as he stands facing me.

"I'm not here to hurt you or fight you," I try to reason with him as he stalks toward me once more, studying me almost as if thinking it through.

I see the blade too late as it flies toward me.

Sweet Vengeance

Oh shit. I feel the stinging pain as it grazes past my face, warm blood dripping from the fresh wound.

He sprints at me, and I quickly dodge, rolling out of the way. The wig slips off my head as I roll to a standing position. My dark hair flows past my shoulders from its loose hold.

Shit, no!

I turn to face the unyielding man and find him staring at me in shock.

"You're the girl from earlier," he says. "I should have known."

Quickly overcoming the shock, he throws another blade at me; this one, I catch midair by the back of the blade and hurl it back at him. It bites into his thigh, causing him to gasp in pain. Grabbing the blade's hilt, he jerks it out of his flesh with a groan, glaring at me before sprinting forward, his weapon aimed at me. I sidestep him, turning and grabbing his arm, when I hear a loud snap followed by a scream of agony. I look up at his pained face in shock, realizing that I just broke his arm.

My heart compresses as guilt floods through me. *I can't believe I hurt the guy who helped and never did anything to me.*

He spins, and his fist collides with my stomach.

Fuck that. Quickly regaining my composure, I grab his unbroken arm, turning and dropping my weight again. He lands hard on his back. Letting go, I back away slowly as I watch him roll over and struggle to stand. With a blade in his outstretched hand, he weakly glares at me.

"I will not die here, not by your hand," he slurs as his injuries start to overtake him.

I watch in horror as he collapses, his body going still.

Did... Did I just kill him? I question myself as guilt floods me. I try to see if he is breathing as I slowly inch toward him. When I see the soft rise and fall of his back, I breathe a sigh of relief.

Kneeling down next to him, I hold out my hand an inch over his body. I watch as the soft golden glow flows from my hand into his skin. Closing my eyes, I envision the light mending his broken arm to normal and sewing the torn flesh together. I pull my hand just shy of healing him completely, enough to make him feel bruised. Opening my eyes, I check to make sure his injuries are healed.

I look around the park before looking back down at his body, knowing he won't be awake for a few hours. *I don't want to leave him out here. What if the dealer comes back looking for him?* I scan the parking lot for any vehicles before searching his pockets, hoping to find car keys.

The first pocket has his wallet, which I quickly return. In the second pocket, I pull out a set of keys and find a Chevy key on his key chain. Pressing the unlock button, I stand, looking at the parking lot. I see two flashes of amber lights from the back corner, covered by darkness.

Thank God. I kneel down, slinging his arm over my shoulders and lifting him from the ground. I half carry him to the vehicle tucked away in the dark.

I admire the black Camaro as I struggle to get him in the passenger seat. I sit him down gently on the red leather, bend to pick up his legs and place them in the car. Once I have him inside, I walk around to the driver-side door.

Sweet Vengeance

He would kill me for driving his car, but at least he wouldn't end up dead.

I battle with myself internally as I open the door, sliding onto the leather seat and glancing over at his unconscious form as I shut the door. Taking a deep breath, I slide the key into the ignition, turning it; the car purrs to life. Pulling out of the parking spot, I drive toward town to a local hotel.

I park the car in the hotel parking lot and head inside, leaving him in the car. At the counter, a brunette greets me with circles under her eyes sipping on a coffee.

"Hi, I need to book a room," I tell her softly, pulling out my ID and credit card starting to feel exhausted.

She looks at her computer screen. "Will a standard bed work?" she asks me, glancing over the screen to meet my gaze.

"Yes," I tell her as I hand her my card and ID. She takes them and types the information into the computer. Luckily, Jay helped me get a name change, but I could never figure out how he could do it without all the paperwork.

I glance out at the car to find Alarik still passed out.

"Your room number is one-thirty," she tells me as she slides a piece of paper for me to sign and my cards back. She swipes the room key in the scanner before handing it to me.

"Have a good night," she says as I turn to leave.

"Thank you. You try to as well," I say as I walk out the door.

Violet S.R. Cox

Getting back into the car, I drive further into the parking lot and park in front of the assigned room number. I take a deep breath, turn the car off, and step out. I walk up to the room, slip the key card into the slot, unlock it, and open it. I glance around the typical hotel room. The walls are a tannish color. A television sits across from a bed made with a green quilt, the sofa is placed close to the window with a brown coffee table in front of it, and there's a desk with a lamp on it against the wall nearest the entrance. I turn, leaving the door open as I walk to the passenger side door.

Opening it, I gently drape his arm over my shoulders again as I drag Alarik out of the car. He isn't too heavy, but I struggle a bit to get him in the room. Eventually, I lay him gently on the green quilted bed. Leaving the hotel key card and his keys on the nightstand, I shut the curtains and turn the AC on low before I go, shutting the door behind me.

I walk down the sidewalk in front of the hotel and glance back at the door that he is asleep behind before I walk through the dark toward Waterfront Park.

Sweet Vengeance

CHAPTER 7

It's almost one in the morning when I follow the red brick pathway into the park. I pass the concrete monument containing some history of the town. I have stopped to read them once before, but I can't remember what they say for the life of me. I pause, taking in the beautiful scenery before me—looking around the quiet, emptied grass area by the stage, which is well-lit by the many lamp posts and the moon's pale glow, basking everything in its light as if caressing the earth.

As I step off the red bricks and onto the grass, the earthy aroma floods my nostrils, calming my racing thoughts. Passing the stage that the town uses for concerts and festivals, I make my way to one of the dozen swinging benches scattered throughout the park. I return to the red brick path that soon turns into concrete slabs with crushed oyster shells for a splash of color; each slab is outlined and separated by the red brick that matches the rest of the park.

Sitting down, I stare at the black night water the park overlooks. Two heavy chains go into each concrete triangular slab on either side. Concrete, chains, concrete—the pattern repeats, creating a barrier along the water's edge. The chains dip toward the middle as gravity pulls its center down, creating a curve. I watch as the water moves gently from the tide and current, the moon glistening off the small waves.

It's funny how you can forget just how beautiful your hometown is until you actually get out and take it all in. I guess when you live here for so long, you lose the appreciation for its beauty.

I glance over to my left to find the beautiful draw bridge that connects the heart of Downtown Beaufort to Lady's Island. I have no clue why they call it a draw bridge when it doesn't actually lift in the center; the center of this bridge just turns to let sailboats through.

I watch as the bridge's red, white and green lights reflect off the water, painting a beautiful picture. Across from the water of black nothingness, you can see glimmers of lights from distant buildings.

Taking a deep breath as the guilt seeps into me, I lose myself in my thoughts of darkness.

I feel guilty for hurting Alarik. The look on his face, followed by the sound of bone breaking when I broke his arm, flashes in my mind. His scream of pure agony echoes in my soul. How could I hurt someone who helped me? Who was kind to me when no one else was? I know it was self-defense, but he was only human. I shouldn't have used so much force. I could have killed him.

Taking a deep breath, I try to calm my racing thoughts.

Snap! The sound of a twig snapping pulls me from my thoughts. I jump, spinning around toward the noise.

Sweet Vengeance

My eyes meet Alarik's stormy-blue ones. The only sign of our fight is the hole in his black jeans. He stands there studying me carefully, and I swallow past the lump in my throat.

"I'm sorry. I don't want to fight," I say in a rush, causing him to raise an eyebrow. "I'm just... going to leave."

"Hold on," I hear him say as I turn to leave. His hand wraps around my upper arms, not too rigid, but enough to send flashbacks from the night of the rape. My breathing comes in a harsh wave.

"Please, please let go of my arm," I plead, trying to regain control of my emotions and push the painful flashback away.

I feel his hand slip from my arm.

"Sorry," I mutter as I turn to face him. He shrugs and steps back.

"How much do I owe you for the room?" he asks me. "I am assuming you are the one who took me there." I awkwardly wrap my arms around myself as I nod, waves of guilt crashing into me.

"Please, don't worry about it. I... didn't mean to hurt you, Rik," I explain. "It was the least I could do is make sure you were safe in case the drug dealer came back looking for you."

He studies me carefully as if he is trying to figure me out. "Where did you learn to fight?"

"My father," I admit. "He trained me." I shrug, glancing everywhere to avoid meeting his eyes.

"Okay, I guess that would explain a lot," he says. "But what I don't understand is why you were at the park to begin with. Were you stalking your ex?"

"Something like that, but that is between him and I," I tell him, meeting his eyes. "Why do you hate him?"

"That is none of your business," he says coldly. "Now, what is your real name? I am assuming it's not Claire."

I shake my head. "My real name is Se—"

"Scarlett, is that you?" I hear the voice of the man from my nightmares say from behind me.

Rik glances over my shoulder, tensing before his eyes return to mine. I catch my breath as I start to tremble slightly. My heart races as I take a deep breath to calm myself.

I meet Rik's eyes before I turn to face Abe, praying that Rik won't attack me while my back is turned.

"It is you," Abe says, smiling, but his chocolate eyes reveal surprise; he seems bulkier, dressed in a wrinkled red shirt and khaki shorts, his shaggy blonde hair slipping into his face slightly.

"What do you want?" I ask, annoyed.

"Aren't you a sight for sore eyes," he says as he stops before me.

I fight the urge to take a step back. I feel Rik's presence as he steps closer behind me. *Please, don't let this be some type of tag team thing.* Abe's eyes go behind me to Rik, who hasn't said anything. Glancing back at him, I notice his hands forming into fists as he glares at Abe.

"I think it's best if you leave us alone," I say as I return my gaze back to Abe, who is smirking, which immediately drops at what I just said. I fight the urge to squirm under his cold stare as his eyes meet mine.

"Is that how you thank someone who showed you a great time?" he asks coldly. "How about showing some respect." He steps closer, looming over me by two inches. Anger sparks deep within me.

"You call that a great time?" I demanded, glaring up at him. He grabs me by my shoulders, bringing me against his hard chest. The fear slams into me, and I lose all my training instincts. I am frozen like a deer in headlights.

"Listen here, you ungrateful little bitch. You enjoyed every second of it, and you know it. How about being a little grateful?" he growls as he moves a strand of hair away from my face. His fingertips brushing against my cheek sends chills through my body.

"LET GO OF ME!" I demand as I try to pull away from him, but his grip on my arm only tightens.

"She said let go," Rik says from behind me, his voice ice cold.

Glancing back at him, I notice he is visibly shaking, and his hands are tightly formed into fists as he glares at Abe. I hear the amused chuckle as Abe spins me around; my back is against his chest, and I am facing Rik.

Violet S.R. Cox

"You want my leftovers?" Abe asks as he leans toward my neck; his hand snakes around my throat as they stare off. "I will tell you that she is amazing. Have you seen the tattoo on her hip yet?" Before me, Rik is fuming.

I hear the soft laugh escape my mouth, which earns me two glares. "Has he seen it?" I ask.

"Yeah. What's so funny?" Abe growls.

I meet Rik's gaze as I mouth *play along*.

"He's the one who went with me and paid for it," I say as I stare at Rik, who smiles. "Which reminds me, did I ever pay off my debt?"

"Yeah. Best payment I ever got," he says, looking up at Abe, who has loosened his grip on me.

"You… you cheated on me?" he asks, sounding shocked and hurt.

"Did you really not know?" Rik asks, sounding surprised.

I bring my elbow forward and slam it back into Abe's stomach, causing him to release me. I sprint forward, but his hand wraps around my wrist, spinning me to face him. I feel the stinging pain of his palm against my cheek, blurring my vision with tears as I fall to the ground. I stand up, feeling the red outline of his handprint forming on my cheek. Angry, I step toward him when a hand softly grabs my arm, pulling me to a stop.

"He's not worth it," Rik whispers beside me as he gently pushes me behind him, protectively positioning himself between Abe and me. "He is nothing but scum," he adds, his voice dripping with venom.

Sweet Vengeance

Abe growls before roughly grabbing Rik by the front of his shirt. *Think. Think.* I shout mentally to myself. *Phone.* I quickly search my pockets for my cell phone, pulling it out as I eye both men. My fingers glide over the screen before placing it against my ear.

"There is a guy here harassing and assaulting people," I say quickly. "The Waterfront Park, by the stage." I try to make my voice sound as panicky as possible as I stare at Abe, who returns a glare, letting go of Rik.

"You just wait, Scarlett," he says threateningly. "He won't always be around to save your ass. Your parents aren't going to be happy when they find out you are alive," he adds before he storms off in the direction he came.

What does he mean my parents aren't going to be happy? Dread fills me as Alarik looks at me, his chest heaving. I pull the phone away from my ear and shove it back into my pocket.

"Was your phone even on?" he asks curiously. I shake my head.

"Nope, but he didn't know that," I tell him, trying to smile through the anxiety attack currently fighting to break the surface. I hear his soft chuckle as he shakes his head in amusement, and I see a smile form on his lips for the first time.

"Why don't you take a seat?" he asks me, gesturing toward the bench swing. "I promise not to start anything," he adds as if sensing my hesitation.

Alarik sits on one side, and I carefully sit on the other. We linger in silence, our eyes glancing around the park as we try to process what happened.

"So, your name is Scarlett?" he asks, his eyes finding mine; I immediately look away, trying to find my voice.

"It used to be."

"What do you mean 'used to be'?" he asks.

I meet his eyes, taking a deep breath, trying to suppress my feelings. "I changed it. My real name is Selen."

"I think it suits you better," he tells me.

I have a flashback to the hallway years ago.

"Thank you," I say as silence fills the air around us.

"How did you know that people call me Rik?" he asks, studying me as he waits for an answer.

"We have met before. Years ago," I admit, briefly meeting his eyes before returning my gaze to the water.

"We have?" he asks as he tries to think. "When and where?"

"School," I answer. "I was the girl that you stopped to help in the hallway. You helped me pick up my books, even carried them to our next class."

His eyes go wide, and his jaw drops as the realization sinks in.

"You were the girl who ran off," he says.

I laugh at the lie that my parents told about my disappearance. They just assumed I ran away.

Sweet Vengeance

"I didn't exactly run away. I have been here the whole time, just lying low," I explain, shrugging as I watch the dark waves overlap one another as if playing tag.

"But why?"

"Let's just say I had no choice," I mumble. "It's nothing against you, but it's very personal, and I am not ready to share that quite yet." He nods in understanding. "Any idea what time it is?"

He glances down at his watch. "Almost three."

"I really should head home," I say as I stand up. Turning to look at him, I add, "I really am sorry for almost killing you."

"Hey, look, just stay out of my way," he says as I walk away.

I head to the park exit, stepping onto the sidewalk on the main road. The street is deserted, looking like a ghost town.

"Scarlett," the cruel voice calls from behind me.

CHAPTER 8

The voice of my rapist causes me to freeze, sending chills down my spine. My breath hitches out of fear. I gulp past the lump in my throat before looking down the sidewalk to find him a few yards away from me, a smile plastered on his face. A horrible tremble ripples through my body.

"Did you really think you could get rid of me that easily?" he questions as he steps forward; I shadow his movement and step back. *Think of a way out.* As I recall all the escape routes, I try to choose the best one.

"Why can't you just leave me alone?" I beg shakily, which causes his smile to grow. *Damn It. Why not just tell him that you are terrified of him? Dumb ass.* I chastise myself for studying him.

"I can't do that."

"Why not?" I ask as I place one foot behind the other.

Sweet Vengeance

"Have you really not figured that out yet?" he chuckles.

"Figured *what* out?"

"You see, I only asked you out because your parents got bored of you and wanted you gone. They knew you had a crush on me and paid me to take care of their little problem," he says, gesturing at me. "And you fell right for it, hook, line, and sinker."

I stop, shocked. *My own parents sold me out?* I mean, yeah, they were abusive and hated me because they had me at sixteen. *But to hire someone to kill me?*

I catch my breath as I recall that night, and everything clicks into place.

My dad passed Abe a handful of cash, smiling as I walked down the steps in my long, pale blue dress, excited for the night that every girl dreamed of.

"Take care of her," my father told him, smiling before glancing up at me. His face was devoid of emotion as he fixed me with a cold stare. Abe nodded in agreement and gestured for me to come, taking my hand as my father opened the door for us.

"Remember our agreement," my father told Abe as we stepped over the threshold.

God, I was so stupid.

"I'll make sure you're dead this time," Abe says coldly, snapping me back to the present. He comes to a stop before me, smiling. "Or I could lock you up and make you my plaything."

Violet S.R. Cox

My stomach ties into knots at the thought. I step back as he launches himself forward, grabbing my shoulders. I bring my knee up into his groin and he falls to the ground, clutching his manhood and groaning in agony.

"Fucking... bitch!" he growls out through pained moans as I spin on my heels and dart across the narrow street. I glance back to see him pulling himself to his feet. I keep running. Heavy steps thud behind me as he follows, and I dash into a small alley.

"SCARLETT!" His voice echoes off the brick walls as I run through it to the dead end.

Fuck. Fuck... Shit!

I stare at the brick wall towering before me. I hear every thud of his footsteps getting closer as I frantically look around the dark alley. My eyes land on a ladder that leads to the roof; it is my only option for escape.

Running to it, I start climbing as fast as I can. The soft clinking of feet against the metal surrounds me as I reach the roof. Panting, I look to scan the flat concrete area, glancing back down and realizing Abe is about halfway up the ladder.

Think, damn it. Think!

My only option is risky. I look back at the ladder as Abe nears the top. Without a second thought, I sprint toward the roof's edge and propel myself across the space separating the buildings, feeling my feet leave the ground for a split second before I stumble onto the lowered roof. My ankle goes sideways as I land hard, causing me to lose my balance, rolling until I'm stopped by something hard slamming into my back, knocking the breath out of me.

Sweet Vengeance

Fighting to breathe, I glance behind me to find a brick wall.

I hear a loud thud. Looking at the roof's edge, Abe slowly stands from a crouch, reminding me of a horror movie. His eyes land on mine as he stands straight and stalks across the roof between us. I push myself to my feet and nearly collapse when I put pressure on my right ankle. Pain shoots through my leg.

Gritting my teeth, I turn and hobble across the roof away from him, trying to make it to the next building. I stop at the edge, staring at the space between the buildings, knowing it is too far to jump with my injury.

"Guess you have nowhere else to run to now," Abe says coldly as he stops behind me.

I turn, facing him as he closes the distance between us. My foot hits the edge.

Abe's hand wraps around my throat, pulling me away from the edge. I pound my fist against his chest as he pushes me against the hard wall, lifting me off the ground. He slams my head into the bricks, sending a blinding pain throbbing through my skull and bright white dots dancing through my vision. I gasp for breath as I sluggishly slap his arms, trying to break his hold. My arms start to feel heavy with each passing second of being deprived of oxygen.

Guess this is how I die.

Suddenly, his hand is gone from my throat, and I land softly on my feet, grabbing my neck as I inhale the fresh oxygen. I glance at him.

"You aren't going to win this," he says.

I feel the blinding pain of his palm against my cheek, the force from it sending me to my hands and knees.

"That is for running from me. This—" his foot collides with my side, sending a new wave of pain exploding through me "—is just for being a bitch." He swings his foot back into my side again. I cry in pain as I land on my back from the force.

Staring up at him, I see a shadow launch into him out of nowhere, tackling him to the ground.

What the?

I hear the sound of grunts and fighting. I roll onto my side, wincing in pain as I watch two figures wrestle against each other a few feet away; their moves blur as I fight the darkness dancing in my vision. One falls to the ground, and the other darts toward me.

Guess this is it.

"Selen," I hear the panic in the familiar voice. I meet his stormy blue eyes in a daze.

"Rik?" I ask weakly. *How did he know?*

I see a shadow emerge behind him as Abe stalks closer. My eyes go wide.

"BEHIND YOU!" I shout through the pain, trying to warn him.

Sweet Vengeance

He spins to a standing position before his attacker. I watch in horror as Abe's fist collides with his face, sending him to the ground. Alarik lands hard, and I see no movement. Abe chuckles as he stalks toward me.

"Now, where were we before he interrupted the fun we were having?" Abe questions. "Oh, yeah, that's right." He kicks me hard in the stomach. "I was teaching you a lesson."

Kneeling down in front of me, he grabs my shoulder, sitting me up against the brick wall. He gently moves the hair away from my face, his finger stroking my cheek, sending chills through me. The black spots grow more prominent in diameter in my vision, and the pain in my skull throbs.

Grabbing me by the chin, Abe forces me to look up at him. "Why do you always have to do things the—"

CLINK. Abe falls to his side, revealing Rik standing behind him, panting with a metal pipe in his hands. His chest rises and falls as he inhales deeply, his eyes on Abe's motionless body before dropping the pipe to the ground. It hits the concrete rooftop with an echoing clatter, vibrating through my head and causing me to squeeze my eyes against the harsh noise.

"Selen, are you okay?" Rik asks, kneeling down; my eyes fight to adjust to him.

Reaching my hand, I touch the tender spot on the back of my head. Pulling my hand back, I notice my palm is stained with blood. Through all the pain, I somehow look up at him and smile.

"I'm just peachy," I slur.

Violet S.R. Cox

Looking at me with concern, he helps me stand up.

Weird. Why is he worried about me?

I cry out in pain, nearly collapsing when I put pressure on my right ankle. Alarik quickly catches me, putting my arm around his neck, his arm wrapping around my waist as he supports my weight. We round the wall I hit earlier to find a door leading to a stairwell. My head starts to feel heavy.

"Selen, stay awake. Do *not* fall asleep," Rik barks loudly in my ear.

I open my eyes to find us on the sidewalk of the deserted main street.

"We need to get you to the hospital," he says.

"No hospitals," I slur as I fight the strong pull of darkness. "My address is—"

Sweet Vengeance

CHAPTER 9
Alarik's POV

"No hospitals," she slurs. "My address is—" Her voice cuts off as she goes limp with my arm wrapped around her waist. I lean her back to make sure she is still alive.

Shit.

"Selen, Selen. Come on, wake up," I say, watching her chest rise and fall, waiting for a response. She doesn't give one.

Under the street lamps, I notice that the back of her dark hair is sticky and matted with drying blood. I eye the bruises forming on her body, contrasting with her pale skin and dark hair that partially hid her face from view, reminding me of a broken angel.

Violet S.R. Cox

Where do I take her? I glance around the deserted little town, unsure of where to go. I place my arms under her fragile, abused body, carrying her with her head against my shoulder. The usual buzzing town is silent; the only sound is my footsteps against the pavement and our breathing as I turn the corner.

I am hyper-aware of every breath she takes as I return to the parking lot. My car sits in the darkest parking space, and as I approach my solid black Camaro, I quickly scan my surroundings. Once at the passenger door, I set her feet on the ground as I balance her weight, opening the car door. I carefully placed her on the leather seats. I can't seem to peel my eyes away from her. Taking a deep breath, I shut the car door and walked to the driver's side.

Sliding onto the leather seats, I slip the key into the ignition and turn it, making the car purr to life. Glancing over at Selen as I pull out of the dark parking spot, I drive out onto the main street and try to think of the best place to take her. I don't want to put her in the hotel, just in case Abe sees me leave her. He would likely try to break into the room to cause more harm.

Why am I feeling protective of her? The random lights from the street and a passing gas station dance in the cab briefly as I drive into the darkness. I hear the soft melody surrounding me as I get lost in my thoughts.

Why was she after Abe? What happened between them? Why is she terrified of him? When he came close, she froze up and couldn't fight at her full potential, which I have witnessed before. What is so different about her? I can't quite figure it out.

I return my eyes to the road as I turn right, pulling onto the gravel that leads up to my house. Hoping I am not making a mistake by bringing her, I park the car in my usual spot, shut it off, and step out. I approach the passenger side, open it, and lift her body carefully out. As I step onto the front porch, the exterior light casts us in its glow.

I carefully get her inside and place her on the couch. I gently move her head to the side, checking her wound. The hair is still caked with blood, but I don't find an injury.

Weird. What about her ribs? I pull her shirt up just enough to check her stomach and ribs, finding them faintly bruised, almost like her body has already healed most of the way. *Not possible.* Respectfully pulling her shirt down, I grab the black blanket off the back of the couch, gently covering her with it.

Whatever she has gone through, she is fighting the trauma.

Taking a deep breath, I go to my bedroom to shower and change into clean clothes.

Turning on the shower, I recall the moment she mentioned earlier.

I'm in the hallway of our school, heading to second period. I notice a girl with dark shoulder-length hair kneeling to pick up her pile of books that a football player just knocked out of her hands. Shaking my head, I watch the students step around her, not stopping to offer help. I kneel before her, helping her retrieve her books, which surprises her. I stand and offer my hand, pulling her up.

"Thank you," she shyly says as her bright green eyes meet mine, nearly taking my breath away.

I remember her now. She was the one who always drew in class. She never spoke unless spoken to and always seemed to limp as if always slightly in pain.

Violet S.R. Cox

Pulling myself back to the present, I finish showering and get dressed.

Chapter 10

My dad raises his hand for the third time tonight. I cringe and try to back peddle from him, but his open palm comes speeding toward me. I feel the harsh sting on my cheek, causing me to fall backward. Pain shoots through my body as my back collides with the corner of the solid wooden coffee table. Gritting my teeth in agony, trying to keep from crying.

I look at my father, who is hovering over me, yelling.

"This house is a mess. I told you to clean it!" he rants. "You are useless and a waste of space. Go to your room." He storms out, walking into the kitchen.

I grimace as I pull myself off the gray carpet. Limping up the stairs, which match the living room's floor, I make it to my bedroom door in pure agony. I stagger inside, shutting the door behind me as tears flood my vision and I collapse onto my bed.

Violet S.R. Cox

Nothing I ever do is good enough. I always did what I was told, but Dad always found a reason to hit me. Tonight's beating was because I wasn't folding laundry fast enough and hadn't cleaned the dishes yet.

Why do they hate me so much? What have I ever done to them?

A knock at my door interrupts my pitiful thoughts. I limp over to the door, gradually opening it to find a guy with shaggy blonde hair and his chocolate brown eyes meeting mine through the door's crack.

"Abe?" I ask, surprised. I notice my dad standing behind him with his arms crossed over his chest.

"He has a question he wants to ask you," my father states before walking back downstairs.

I turn my eyes back to the quarterback who stands before me. I open my door, letting him into my plain room consisting of only a bed, desk, and dresser. Stepping in, he crosses the room and sits at the foot of the bed. I close my door as he scans the space. I turn to face him, baffled.

Why was he here? He has never noticed me before. Why now?

"Scarlett, I came by to ask you if you will go to prom with me?" he asks, shocking me.

"I, um... would have to ask my father first," I explain nervously. My father, for sure, would tell me no. I wasn't allowed a moment of fun or happiness.

"I already asked him, and he said he was fine with it," Abe tells me as he admires me. I feel the heat in my cheeks as a blush creeps in.

Sweet Vengeance

"Oh, um, yeah, it sounds like fun," I answer.

Smiling, he stands up from the bed and walks over to me.

"Plus, I was also wondering if you would be my girlfriend too?" he asks.

I am speechless, and I nod yes as I stare into his eyes as he stops before me. He's only a few inches taller than I am. To my surprise, he gently lifts my chin with his middle and pointer finger. Leaning down, he presses his lips softly against mine. It was how every girl would imagine their first kiss, leaving me speechless.

"I'll see you at school tomorrow, darling," he says after he pulls back, smiling softly. He gently brushes a strand of my dark hair out of my face.

I can't believe it. I have a date for the prom, with the quarterback of all people.

"Sounds good to me," I say, smiling up at him, almost breathless.

He opens the bedroom door, waving goodbye as he enters the hallway. I sit on my bed in shock and hear the steps fade as he leaves. I touch my lips, unsure if I was dreaming or not.

"Scarlett Sirus!" I hear my father shout from downstairs.

Oh shit, what now? My smile vanishes as I creep my way down the stairs, stopping on the last step where my father is standing, waiting for me.

"Yes, sir?" I ask, my eyes glued to the floor, afraid of meeting his gaze.

Violet S.R. Cox

"Here is some money," he says sternly, handing me some folded cash. I look up at him, confused. "That way, you can buy a dress. Go tomorrow after school. You have until five to be home."

"Yes, sir, thank you," I reply in shock, staring down at the money in my hand. He nods emotionless before walking away.

I walk back up to my room. What has gotten into him? Has he had a change of heart?

Still confused, I get ready for bed.

The following day, I stroll into school, rushing to my locker. I turn the combination, unlock it and open it. I grab two textbooks and notebooks out before closing the door. Suddenly, I find Abe leaning against the locker beside mine, startling me.

"Good morning, darling." he greets me with a charming smile that makes me weak at the knees. I can feel the weight of eyes on us as students watch us curiously. I let my hair fall into my face as the blush creeps into my cheeks.

"Morning," I greet back, peeking up at him through my curtain of hair. Gently reaching his hand out, he tucks my hair behind my ear, smiling, amused with my reaction.

I awake to a throbbing headache, lying there unmoving for a moment, thinking about the dream.

Why was I so naive?

Sweet Vengeance

I slowly sit up, pain shooting through my whole body, causing me to groan. I look around the foreign living room that I woke up in.

Where am I? I scan my surroundings, confused. A black coffee table in front of me is littered with a few soda cans and three Xbox controllers. *Well, that's definitely not mine.* The beige wall across from me holds a colossal television that takes up most of the space. The L-shaped couch I'm resting on is dark gray.

I push myself off the sofa and cry in pain as my ankle protests at the sudden weight.

Hearing footsteps thudding softly against the floor, I reach for my weapons to find them gone. *Fuck.* I glance around in a panic, searching for them; my eyes land on a table tucked away in the corner to see my weapons sitting on it. I take a step toward the table.

"Don't."

A familiar voice stops me in my tracks. Alarik leans against the wall, black hair still dripping wet, studying me. My eyes dart back to my weapons and then back to him.

"How do I know I can trust you?" I ask, unsure.

"You can't, and you really shouldn't," he replies, crossing his arms. "But if I really wanted to kill you, I would have done it while you were passed out." His stormy-blue eyes stay focused on me; I can see a hidden spark of kindness deep inside them.

Carefully limping my way back to the couch, I sit down nervously, easing the throbbing pain in my ankle. Alarik sits in the matching recliner off to the side.

Leaning down, I check the condition of my ankle while keeping him in my field of vision.

"How are you feeling?" he asks me; looking up, I find him studying my every move. I sit up straight, my elbows on my knees, as I lean my throbbing head into my hands.

"I've been better," I reply. "What happened?" Everything is still hazy to me, and I am unable to process it with the pounding headache.

He looks at the floor before his stormy-blue eyes meet mine. "You passed out from your injuries that Abe caused," he explains. "You made a stupid move. Why would you take the fight to the rooftops and then back yourself into a corner?" he questions harshly. I look up at him in embarrassment. "You almost got yourself killed."

"I admit it was a stupid move. But I wasn't planning on fighting. I was just trying to get away from him," I answer, finally beginning to recall the events of last night. "I ran into a dead end and had no other option but to go up."

I grit my teeth against the pain in my skull. Standing up, he opens a drawer and tosses me a bottle of pain relievers, then disappears briefly before returning with a bottle of water handing it to me. I take two capsules with a swig of water.

"Thank you," I say, tossing the bottle back to him, which he quickly catches.

"How did that work out for you?" he asks as he sits in the recliner.

Sweet Vengeance

"Well, considering I almost got myself killed, I would say it worked out great. Wouldn't you?" I sarcastically say, which earns me an unamused look. "But, how did you know I was in danger?"

"I heard him yelling your old name," he explains, his eyes searching mine.

A buzzing sound interrupts us; I glance around and back at him, confused.

"That would be your cell phone. I figured I would charge it for you," he says, pointing a few feet from me.

Standing up, I hobble over to where the phone lies charging and unplug it. I look at all the missed calls: ten, all from Jay, along with a few dozen texts. I scroll through the messages of him asking if I was okay, demanding where I was, and demanding me to call him immediately. *Ah fuck.* I feel Alarik's eyes on me.

"Is everything okay?" he asks, seeing the look on my face. Glancing up at Rik, I text Jay, telling him I am okay and will be home shortly.

"It will be, but I have to get home. My dad is kind of freaking out," I answer. Alarik nods in understanding as he pushes himself out of the recliner.

"I'll give you a ride home," he volunteers.

"That'll be greatly appreciated," I tell him as I tuck my phone into my pocket, grab my boots, and slip them on as he does the same with his shoes. He grabs my weapons from the table, handing them to me as he leads the way outside to his car.

Violet S.R. Cox

As he pulls out of his gravel driveway, I stare out the window, watching the trees blur by as we pass; the sound of a rock song plays on the radio as I lose myself in my own thoughts.

"Selen," he calls my name, snapping me back to reality. I look over at him. "You are home," he says, pointing at my house. I glance to find the old cabin standing before us.

"Oh, thank you for the ride and for saving me," I tell him as I open the car door.

"Selen, we're even now. Don't think that we're friends. Abe is mine, so don't get in my way," he warns me coldly, meeting his eyes.

"Look, I'm not backing down. Whoever gets him gets him. So, if you want to waste your time on me, then so be it. But Abe will pay one way or another," I tell him, my voice dripping with venom. Surprise passes through his eyes before he nods in agreement.

"Well, good luck then," he tells me as I get out, closing the door behind me.

Alarik drives off, leaving a trail of dust in his wake. I watch the car disappear out of view before I limp up to my front door. Once inside, I look at the stairs and then at the couch. I decide on the couch instead of trying to hobble up the stairs to my room. My head still throbbing, I lay down on the sofa. Draping the crook of my arm over my eyes, I start dozing off when the loud bang of the front door being slammed shut causes me to jump.

"Where the hell were you?" Jay demands.

Sweet Vengeance

Luckily, my throbbing headache had begun to subside. Taking a deep breath before removing my arm from my face, I glance over at him as I sit up.

"And who the hell was that?" he questions. "What the hell happened?"

I look up at him, waiting for him to finish, when he won't give me a chance to reply. He paces in front of the glass coffee table that separates us, eyeing me sternly.

"Which question would you like me to answer first?" I ask more harshly than I should have, thanks to the pain and aggravation. He stops and actually looks at me, his eyes scanning my body with concern and a hint of anger.

I feel the buzzing sound inside my head, like bees swarming me, which only happens when he is trying to push through the barrier inside my mind. He knew I hated it when he read my mind; it always made me feel violated.

My eyes narrow on his. The heat spreads through me as my temper spikes from annoyance.

"Are you serious right now?" I demand, my voice rising in anger. "Did you really just try to push your way into my mind? I had my ass handed to me on a silver platter by Abe. Another guy saved me. I was so badly injured that I passed out, and he took me to his house to recover." When I finish, I'm practically shouting at him.

"Who was the guy?" he questions.

"Alarik Ashwood. I went to school with him years ago," I tell him. I notice the flash of surprise briefly surface before it vanishes. He stays silent for a few moments before regaining his composure.

"You need to stay away from Alarik," he says, his voice filled with emotional pain. I look up at him, piecing it together.

"Is he?" I question.

He simply nods his head. I watch as the emotion vanishes, replaced by a stern Jay.

"You should have come home immediately, and none of this would have happened." he preaches to me.

"If I came home, Abe would know where I live," I tell him, trying to remain calm as he flashes me an angry look.

"It's your *own* fault. You put yourself in danger. I have trained you, and *yet* you are still useless."

"I can't believe you just said that to me," I reply, my voice sounding broken as the shock and hurt of his words fills me.

"It's the truth," he states coldly before leaving. The door slams shut behind him with a loud bang.

I stare at the door he just vanished through, tears streaming down my cheek. Angrily wiping them away, I stand up, limping to the closet, where I grab my emergency duffle and sling it over my shoulder. I slowly make it to the door, grabbing my wallet off the table. I take one more glance at the living room before I turn the doorknob and step out onto the porch.

Chapter 11

A small startled yelp leaves my lips as I turn, bumping into someone—my right ankle protests as I step sideways. I feel myself falling, but to my surprise, I don't hit the ground. I glance at the hand that catches me, confused.

"Are you okay?" Alarik asks, helping me stand. He studies me, concerned, and glances down at my ankle.

"Yeah, yeah. I'm fine," I lie, knowing my eyes are red and swollen. I quickly look away, heading for the gray porch that has seen better days.

"No, you aren't. You're crying."

"No, no. I'm fine." Embarrassed, I insist, but I'm mostly trying to reassure myself that I'm okay.

I feel his finger under my chin as he gently makes me meet his stormy-blue eyes, studying me with concern. It's as if he is looking into my soul. My breath hitches as I stare back into his eyes.

"If you aren't crying, then why are your eyes red and swollen?" he asks me, worry filling his voice. *Didn't he just say we aren't friends?* "Are you hurt?" His hand drops from my chin, but his eyes never leave mine.

"No, not hurt any more than when you dropped me off. I got something in my eyes," I lie, which causes him to lift his eyebrow, giving me that *oh really* look.

"You know you suck at lying, *right*?" he asks as he leans against the porch railing, his eyes going to the duffle bag at my side. "Are you leaving?"

"Why are you back?" I ask, trying to change the topic away from me.

Alarik reaches into his pocket, pulling out my cell phone. "You left your phone on the passenger seat. That awful ringtone nearly scared me half to death," he says as he hands it back to me. It must have slipped out of my pocket.

"Oh, okay. Thank you," I say as I slip the phone into the duffle. I limp past him and down the steps, but he follows behind me.

"So you're leaving, but where are you going?" he questions.

I stop dead in my tracks, unsure. I haven't planned that far ahead yet. I feel the weight of his eyes on my back.

"I guess I will be staying in a hotel for a few nights," I say, shrugging.

Sweet Vengeance

"Why stay at a hotel when you have a house?" he asks.

I glance back at Alarik, trying to get a read off of him, but all I see is his usual uncaring exterior. But I swear there's a look of sympathy deep in his eyes.

"My dad and I got into a heated argument. I just need to get away for a few days, so I'm going to find a cheap room." Though I find myself explaining it to him, for some odd reason, I feel like I can trust him. "Any suggestions of which hotel?" Pulling out my cell phone, I begin to search for Beaufort hotels.

"Uh, I have a crazy idea," he says, causing me to look at him. "How about you just stay at my house? It would be cheaper, and I have a huge house," he says in a rush, glancing around as if embarrassed for suggesting it.

I stare at him in shock and confusion, then take a moment to weigh the pros and cons of the arrangement. He would have a home advantage over me. He did save me, though.

"Maybe we could come to an understanding and work together to get rid of Abe," he adds, which catches my attention.

"You want to team up?" I ask in curious disbelief.

"You don't have to," he says, shrugging. "I'm sorry. It was weird of me to even offer."

"No, you have a point. My thing is, can I trust you not to kill me?" I ask, studying him.

"I don't want to hurt you. I just don't want you getting in the way," he explains. "So, maybe if we get to know each other, we could take our mutual enemy out. For us to do that, we would have to trust each other."

He has some valid points. And it would be easier with a partner.

"Plus, you would kind of have to be alive for it to work," he adds.

I glance up at him as the thought of being used as bait floods my mind. The memory of that night starts to flash in my head.

"Nothing like that, Selen," he quickly adds; he must have seen the look of horror on my face. Taking a deep breath, I push the memories away and meet his eyes as I calm my anxiety.

"You make a valid point," I answer, and he seems momentarily surprised that I would consider it. "Abe wouldn't know what to do with the two of us against him. But are you sure?"

"Yes. I am sure," he answers, his body relaxing slightly. He points to his black Camaro, which sits in the driveway. "Let's go then."

Walking to his car and opening the passenger door, I slide onto the leather seats, placing the duffle on the floorboard. Rik slides into the driver seat, starts the car, and pulls onto the dirt road. We sit in silence, listening to the soft rock music.

A few short minutes later, we pull into his gravel driveway. In front of us stands a huge, light gray two-story house with a solid white front door and windows adorned with navy blue shutters. The enormous front porch wraps around the house with a roof sheltering it, and he pulls to a stop in front of a garage that matches the home's exterior.

Sweet Vengeance

I grab my duffle and exit the car, glancing around at the well-maintained property. I follow Rik to the house in silence as awkwardness kicks in. We walk in a side door that matches the front one. Stepping inside, I notice that we are standing in the kitchen, which is breathtaking.

Every woman would probably kill for this kitchen. It's huge, with plenty of counter space. It's probably the most enormous kitchen I have ever seen. The old rustic gray cabinets are paired with a black granite countertop that takes up about half the kitchen and wraps around into a breakfast bar close to us. Stainless steel bar stools rest under the counter, surrounded by matching stainless steel appliances, a built-in double oven on one wall, an island in the middle, and a glass-top stove. The kitchen sink sits before a window, and the black onyx flooring runs throughout. The mocha walls pair perfectly.

"Wow, this kitchen is amazing," I comment almost silently. I realize he is staring at me and already about halfway down the hallway, waiting. "Sorry," I say, following quickly.

I pass a doorway on the left. As I walk past, I notice it's a laundry room, the walls decorated with newspaper wallpaper. The hallway leads into the living room, revealing the gray couch that I woke up on earlier.

He turns, looking at me. "Why don't you put your duffle down, and I will give you a quick tour of the house," he suggests. I set my duffle on the couch, following him as he leads. "There is a bathroom over there," he tells me, pointing to a small hallway I didn't notice.

"You know where the kitchen is, and we passed the laundry room. There is another way into the kitchen," he explains, pointing at a small room off to the side of the living room, which looks like a dining room. He leads the way to the staircase, gesturing to a door you must pass to get to the stairs on the right.

"This is my room. *Obviously*, it's off limits."

I nod in understanding as he walks to the stairs and stops in front of them. "I won't make you walk up these with your injured ankle. But there are four rooms and two bathrooms up there." He steps a few more feet past the staircase, and I noticed another door on the other side of the stairs that I didn't see before. He opens the door wide.

"This will be your room," he tells me as he moves to the side. I step past him into the vast room and find sapphire blue walls and a king-size bed made with a black comforter. "You have your own bathroom, too," he says, pointing at one of the doors off to the side.

I notice the French doors on the other side of the room; I walk over to them, moving the black curtains to the side, revealing a vast backyard with an in-ground pool in the middle of the lawn.

"Is it okay?" he asks almost nervously.

"Yes, it's more than okay," I tell him as I turn to look at him, still in awe. "Your house is beautiful, and so is the property."

"Just wait until you see the rest of the property," he says. "Once your ankle is healed, I will give you a tour of the grounds. You are more than welcome to the pool and the use of the kitchen."

When he finishes his explanation, Alarik vanishes out of the doorway. He returns a few moments later carrying my duffle bag, placing it on the bed for me.

"Thank you."

Sweet Vengeance

"I'll let you settle in. If you need anything, I'll either be in my room or the living room." He nods his head as he makes his way to the bedroom door. Stopping on the threshold, he turns to look at me. "The door locks from the inside," he adds as he closes it behind him.

I walk into the bathroom and stare, stunned. It's gorgeous. The walls match the bedroom, and the white vanity is paired with a gray countertop, and gray tile stretches throughout. A shower and tub are set against the wall across from the vanity, while towels and rags sit neatly stacked on a shelf near the shower. I turn the shower on, letting it warm up as I grab clean clothing from my bag.

After showering, feeling human again, I dress in my red plaid pajama pants and red tank top. I step back into the bedroom, unsure of what to do. I head toward the door and turn the knob when I decide to draw instead. I walk to the bed, pull out my sketchbook and pencils, and lay on my stomach atop the covers.

Violet S.R. Cox

CHAPTER 12
Alarik's POV

I wonder what Abe did to her. Whatever happened, it still has her spooked. She loses her fighting instincts when she sees him, which tells me she fears something. It had to be really bad, considering I had never seen fear in those bright eyes before. I recall how she froze when he called her name in the park. The look on her face was one of pure terror. I couldn't hear what he whispered in her ear bug I could see the fear trying to overtake her.

Shaking my head, I look around the living room and realize that the movie I had playing has ended and another one has started. Glancing at the time, I notice that a couple of hours have passed, and I haven't heard anything from Selen, not even a peep since she got into the shower.

I turn the television off, getting up from the couch to head to my bedroom, when I notice her door is cracked open with light shining on the floor. I glance between my door and hers, debating if I should peek in on her to make sure she is alright. I silently approach her door but don't hear any movement or sound inside. Quietly pushing it open, I find her asleep on her stomach on the bed, dressed in red plaid pajama pants and a red tank top, her head on her outstretched arm with a pencil in her hand. Something white lays on the bed in front of her face. Curious, I step into the room.

Yeah, this definitely isn't stalkerish at all.

Stopping at the edge of the bed, I realize she was drawing when she fell asleep. I pick up the sketchbook, careful not to wake her, glancing down at her slender body stretched across the bed. Her long dark hair partially covers her face from view, though her eyelids are closed, hiding those beautiful jade-green eyes that seem to look through you. She reminds me of what an angel would look like sleeping; a very deadly angel with her fighting skills.

Tearing my eyes away from her sleeping form, I look down at the sketchbook to find myself staring back at me from the page, my hand outstretched with a blade coming at me. The detail is so realistic that it looks like the knife will come right off the paper. I turn the page to the one before to find a deer in a field with trees in the background. The shading and little details make it seem like I am actually there. I never took her for an artist, but the drawings are superb; she had some real talent.

I return to the drawing she was working on, softly placing the book back on the bed. She moves her head, readjusting it, causing me to panic momentarily. I might freak her out if she woke to find me standing beside the bed. Grabbing a throw she must have placed to the side, I drape it over her before exiting her room.

I don't know why, but I feel this need to protect her.

Silently shutting the door behind me I cross the hall to my own bedroom, which is diagonal to hers. I step in and walk to the bathroom, deciding to take a shower.

After showering, I am pulling a pair of flannel pajama bottoms on when a scream shatters the silence; echoing through the house, causing my head to jerk up at the cries of fear. I bolt toward Selen's room, filled with worry that she is hurt. Pushing the door open, I find her still asleep, tossing and turning, knocking her sketchbook and pencils to the floor. I dart to the bed when I realize she is having a nightmare, whimpering between her terrible screams.

"Selen!" I call her name, gently shaking her as I sit on the bed. "Selen, wake up!" I raise my voice, trying to wake her.

Suddenly, the screams stop. Her eyes snap open, fear still in them, and her breathing hitches as she bolts to a sitting position. She searches the room, trembling.

"Are you okay?" I ask. Her eyes land on mine as she pulls her knees up to her chest, arms wrapped around them, dropping her head on her arms.

"I'll be fine," she mumbles. "I'm sorry if I woke you." An embarrassed flush creeps onto her cheeks. "I... I get night terrors," she explains as her hair falls in her face like a curtain.

Reaching out without thinking, I gently stroke her hair out of her face, tucking it behind her ear. "It happens to the best of us," I tell her, knowing just how terrible they are from experience.

She stands up from the bed, walking to the French door, shaking her arms as if to chase the nightmare away. She glances out the window before pacing back and forth, no longer limping. *How did she heal so fast?* She was barely able to walk on it a few hours ago.

She walks back to the French doors, unlocking them and stepping out on the porch and into the fresh air. I follow her out, too worried to leave her alone. I notice her staring at the pool as her breathing evens out.

"Do you have a swimsuit?" I ask her, causing her to meet my eyes.

"Yeah. Why?"

"Go get changed, and let's go for a swim. It'll help ease your mind and chase the nightmare away," I say before going to change myself.

After changing, I leave my French doors and find her sitting by the pool in a violet bikini that shows off all her curves, with her feet dangling in the water. The moonlight basks her in its glow, reflecting off her shiny dark hair creating the look of an angelic halo.

CHAPTER 13

My feet dangle in the water as I sit on the pool's edge, waiting for Rik to return, lost in thought. His eyes were so concerned when he woke me from the nightmare.

I hear soft footsteps and glance over my shoulder to find Alarik strolling toward the pool, wearing black trunks. His dark hair is out of its usual braid and falls in soft waves to his chin, giving him that darkly mysterious look. I catch my breath at the sight of his bare chest. He was muscular in all the right places.

Realizing that I am staring, I peel my eyes away from him and back to the gleaming water that reflects the moonlight.

"How's the water?" he asks, sitting beside me.

"It feels great," I answer.

Sweet Vengeance

He dips his feet in the water and lets out a sigh of relief. "Yes, it does," he says, looking back at me. When he meets my eyes, I find myself admiring him again.

Silence falls between us, but it's oddly comforting. I look around the moonlit yard as I try to avoid the feelings of attraction, the wanting to run my fingers through his hair.

He doesn't like you like that. Plus, have you not learned anything? I chastise myself.

"So I was thinking about how we could take Abe out." Alarik's voice breaks the silence. "We have to get to know each other and learn each other's fighting skills," he explains nervously.

"Okay, what do you want to know?" I ask, meeting his eyes.

"Well, I think we both need to know why each of us is after him," he continues softly. "I'll explain first, and hopefully that'll make you little more comfortable with sharing your story. I can tell this is going to be hard on you."

"Yes, it will be," I admit, glancing nervously at the water, "but you're right. We need to know each others reason for going after him."

"I had a best friend who was a girl. Her name was Grace," he begins. "She was dating Abe for a few weeks when he violently raped her. No one believed her when she tried to tell the truth. He got off the hook, and it became too much for her to handle. Eventually, she took her own life." My heart compresses as I watch the brief moment of heartache pass through him, tears threatening to escape his eyes. "Because of that asshole, I lost my bestfriend."

Violet S.R. Cox

"How long ago did this happen?" I ask, my voice filled with sympathy.

His eyes reach mine as he thinks. "About a year ago," he answers as his stare falls onto the water.

"Guess it's my turn," I nervously start, taking a deep breath to calm my racing heart. I turn my eyes to the back corner of the property, where the dark trees meet the grass.

"It was a little over two years ago. Abe came to my house asking me to be his girlfriend and his date to the prom. Everything was going so perfectly. You know, a dream come true for a girl; he was so sweet and gentle." I feel the tears coming and steady my breathing.

"After we left the prom, he took a detour down a road I had never been on." I pause again as I take a deep breath to say the words no rape victim ever wants to say. I look at my hands as I nervously pick at my fingers, fidgeting. "Where he raped me. Even after I begged and pleaded." The tears flow down my cheeks.

"Did you ever tell your parents?" he asks me. I shake my head no. "Why not?"

"I found out last night that my abusive father hired Abe to get rid of me," I say numbly. I see the shock cross over his face.

"Your father abused you? That's why you ran away and disappeared," he says. "I am sorry that you had to go through all of that. But it does explain a lot about you." He goes silent. I slowly lower myself into the water to erase the bad memories.

Sweet Vengeance

"You said you and your dad got into a fight earlier."

"He isn't my biological father, but I consider him my dad. He is the guy who saved me that night and also trained me. It may sound stupid and maybe childish, but he got upset with me and called me useless, which is what my real father used to tell me during his daily abuse," I explain as I lean back into the water, soaking my hair. I feel the weight of his gaze as he studies my every move.

"Actually, no, it's not stupid. I understand. You just needed to get away for a bit due to a trigger from the past," he says, meeting my eyes.

I shrug, smiling as I bring my hand through the water, splashing him. His eyes widen in shock before regaining his composed expression, which then turns into a mischievous grin. He stands up, jumps, and lands beside me, his cannonball spraying me with water.

"Ha-ha, payback," he says when he surfaces, a smile painted on his face. A real smile, that looks good on him.

I laugh as I playfully splash him again, which turns into a splashing war. We swim around randomly, splashing each other for about the next hour. When we're finished, I pull myself out of the pool, water dripping as it paints the concrete at my feet.

"I should try to get some sleep before daylight," I tell him muffling a yawn.

"Yeah, me too," he says, climbing out of the pool as well. He walks over to one of the storage benches, pulling out two towels, and hands me one. Thanking him, I take it, wrapping it around my body.

"Thank you for waking me up from the nightmare," I tell him as we make our way back to the house.

"Anytime. I used to have nightmares for the longest time after Grace took her life. So, I know just how traumatizing it can be," he explains as we stop in front of the French doors leading into my bedroom. "Try to get some rest, and I will see you when you wake up."

"Good night."

"Good night, Selen."

I watch as he walks further down the porch and through another set of French doors. I glance at the night sky again before stepping into my bedroom and locking the door behind me.

Walking back to the bathroom, I change out of my wet swimsuit, drape it over the shower, and slip my pajamas back on. I return to the bed, crawling under the covers and melting into the soft mattress, where sleep swallows me.

Chapter 14

  In the morning, I wake up to the sun shining past the curtains. I glance around the quiet room before stretching, swinging my legs over the edge of the bed, and standing. I switch my pajamas out for a loose-fitting shirt and jeans. Pulling the hairbrush through my tangled hair, I braid it out of my face and step out of the bedroom.

  The soft mumble of the television welcomes me as I silently walk to the living room, where I find Rik with an Xbox controller, sitting cross-legged in the oversized recliner, dressed in a black shirt and jeans with his hair freshly braided. I look away from him and at the television as I hear the sound of zombies surrounding his character—he's playing Left 4 Dead. As he shoots the zombies, the graphics start to shake, and the controller vibrates in his hands.

  "Watch out—Tank," I say as I walk around the couch and sit down, causing him to jerk his head in my direction. Surprise fills his face, but I'm unsure if it's because I know the game or because I snuck up on him. Regardless, he returns his eyes back to the game.

"How long have you been there?" he asks as his character throws a Molotov at the Tank, which ignites. I watch as fiery Tank chases after his character.

"Long enough to see that a Smoker got a hold of you," I comment; he glances back at me, surprised. I watch as the Tank finally dies.

"Wait, you know this game?" he asks as he and his team take on another horde of zombies ambushing them.

"Yep," I reply. "I've played it a few times."

He glances back at me as he and his teammates make it to the helicopter, leaving Mercy Hospital. The credits, showing how many zombies were killed, pop up on the television; I begin to read them, but feeling the weight of his eyes on me, I glance over at him, where I find him staring me.

"What?"

"Your hair," he says. "I've never seen it braided before. It looks good."

Surprised by his compliment, I meet his eyes.

"Oh, thank you," I reply as I awkwardly grab the end of my braided hair. "So, um, what's the plan for today?" I ask, trying to switch the subject. He leans back in the recliner, staring at me as he thinks.

"How about we go get breakfast first? I am starving and not much of a cook," he explains.

Sweet Vengeance

"I'll cook if you want me to," I volunteer, momentarily averting my gaze to the floor. "Do you have eggs, bacon, and pancake mix?"

He studies me as if weighing the pros and cons.

"Unless you are afraid of me poisoning you," I joke. A smile spreads across his face as he chuckles, shaking his head no.

"You are welcome to see what I have in the kitchen. I'm kind of curious to see what you can whip up," he says.

Smiling, I stand, running to the kitchen excitedly. "Challenge accepted!" I call over my shoulder. I hear him chuckling behind me as I vanish through the dining room and into the kitchen.

Coming to a stop in front of the stainless steel fridge, I open the door. I find everything I need and take it out, setting it on the black granite countertop. I search the cabinets for pancake mix, eventually finding it, and then hunt for the pots and pans. Then, I start cooking.

I begin with the bacon, the smell filling the kitchen and making my stomach grumble. I pour a line of pancake mix over the sizzling bacon strips. Soft footsteps come into the kitchen as I flip the last bacon pancake.

"Wow, it smells amazing in here," Alarik comments as he sits down at the breakfast bar. I feel the weight of his gaze on me as I turn the stove off and grab two plates. I pile his plate high with bacon, pancakes, and eggs, surprising him as I set it down in front of him.

"You don't have to serve me," he says, but I just shrug and reach for the plate.

"Okay, I guess I *could* take it back then," I say, drawing out the words.

Rik immediately grabs the plate, eyeing me as if daring me to do the just that. I chuckle, walking away, holding the syrup and two glasses of orange juice.

"That's what I thought," I say as I place the stuff before him, turning to make my plate.

I sit across from him as he bites into one of the bacon pancakes. He stops suddenly, looking up at me in surprise.

"This is amazing," he comments through a mouthful of food. I feel the heat spread into my cheeks as I silently eat breakfast.

After we both get our fill, I start cleaning the kitchen, and to my surprise, Rik joins in.

"I got it. You don't have to help," I tell him as he rinses the dishes and places them in the dishwasher.

"You cooked breakfast. You shouldn't have to clean, too," he says as he places the last dish in the dishwasher, closes the door and turns the dial to start it. "Plus, I got a dishwasher," he adds, smiling.

I open the cabinet under the sink, find some surface cleaner and paper towels, and wipe the countertops down. I notice he is leaning against the breakfast bar, watching me curiously, almost as if he's trying to figure me out.

"So, do you want to see the rest of the property?" he asks as I return the cleaner to its proper place. I glance over at him, nodding my head yes.

Sweet Vengeance

"Well, come on, let's go," he says, gesturing for me to follow him.

He opens the door, and we head outside into the summer heat. We pass the swimming pool, and walking toward the woods, I notice the hidden trail.

"So I was thinking," I begin as we walk down the trail, "that we need to learn each other's moves. Maybe we could combine some."

He slows down his pace so that we can walk side by side and says, "That might just work."

"And I need to learn to control the fear that freezes me, making me forget all my training," I mumble as he comes to a stop. I glance around, confused; my eyes land on a punching bag, a pull-up bar, and a few training mats. Everything was built around the trees.

"And in time, you will learn to," he encourages me. I look over at him, surprised to see how caring and understanding he is. "Want to practice a little?" he asks. I nod my head yes in answer.

"But let's make it interesting," I tell him, smiling. His eyes meet mine, nearly taking my breath away as he arches an eyebrow, intrigued.

"What exactly did you have in mind?"

"Well, instead of just the usual training, why don't we make it kind of like a game? Whoever gets three pins first wins. It will help us learn each other's fighting moves," I explain. "Are you up for the challenge?" I cross my arms over my chest, arching my eyebrow at him.

"Challenge accepted," he replies; I can tell by the look in his eyes and the smile on his face that he's going to enjoy this.

We both get into our stances. I make the first move, sprinting toward Rik, stopping just out of reach as he swings his fist through the air. He kicks his leg out, trying to trip me. I jump over it before sweeping my own leg out. Stumbling over it, he falls to the ground; wasting no time, I pin him. His eyes meet mine, and he looks dazed for a brief second.

"Pin one," I tell him as strands of my hair come loose from the braid.

"Not bad," he comments, shoving me off him and jumping to his feet.

I stand as he kicks his foot out at me, which causes me to stumble back and almost lose my balance. Taking advantage of the opening, he tackles me to the ground. The impact knocks the breath out of me momentarily while his body heat is nearly suffocating as it radiates off him.

He gently pins my arms over my head, his legs straddling either side of my body. "Pin," he says, smiling down at me.

"Not bad," I tell him, almost breathlessly; he releases my arms as he stands up, readying himself.

I pull myself off the ground, facing him, when I feel something wet and cold land on me. Looking up at the clouds, it's obvious: rain. I glance back at Rik, who is still staring up at the sky, distracted. I sprint at him, tackling him to the ground and pinning his arms over his head immediately.

"Pin," I say, smiling as his shock turns to a glare.

Sweet Vengeance

"Cheater," he says as the rain starts pounding around us, soaking us in a fury.

"Always expect the unexpected," I tell him as I stand.

Unexpectedly, he launches himself off the ground, catching me off guard as he tackles me. I feel a sharp pain on my thigh as he pins me. He hovers over my body, grinning.

"Pin," he shouts over the pouring rain as he stands up, backing away quickly.

Getting to my feet, I sneak a glance down my thigh, but I don't see anything. My eyes returned to him, determined to get the last pin. I step forward, swinging my fist, which he blocks. His fist swings through the air, and I lean back, avoiding it. I feel the sharp pain burst again through my body, causing me to stumble, but I quickly regain my balance. I meet Rik's eyes as they go wide in shock.

"Selen, are you okay?" he questions me as he points down at my leg.

I am not falling for that. I think he is just trying to distract me until he comes to a standstill, his expression filled with worry.

"Selen, did you, um…" he starts awkwardly. Confused, I stare at him, not understanding what he is trying to say, as his cheeks turn beat red. "Did you start your monthly?"

What? I haven't had a period since becoming immortal. It was definitely one of the pros of immortality: no more painful cramps every month, and it cut down on spending.

"No, what are you talking about?" I ask him, confused. "Why would you think that?"

He points at my leg again. "You're bleeding."

He crosses the space between us as I glance down at my leg to find it wholly soaked red. As I examine my thigh in the cool pouring rain, he comes to my side. "Are you okay?" he asks again.

"Yeah, I think I cut myself on something earlier when you pinned me," I say, standing up straight. "I'll be fine. Let's finish our game."

"Uh, no, let's get you back to the house."

"I'm fine. Let's—"

"No! We are going to see how bad this wound is. Let's go," he says sternly, his face full of worry as he slides one arm around me and helps me back to his house.

Guess there is no arguing with him.

We finally make it back inside, though we're completely drenched. Helping me into the house, he leaves me shivering as the AC wraps around my wet skin. I glance down at my leg to find a hole in my jeans toward the front of my thigh. Rik quickly returns, handing me a towel and one of his huge t-shirts.

"Go dry off real quick. We will throw your clothes in the washer once we get your wound checked out," he instructs as he enters full doctor mode. I nod as I wrap the towel around me, heading toward my room.

Sweet Vengeance

Once there, I strip out of my wet clothes. I glance at the angry gash on my thigh as I pat myself dry before pulling on dry undergarments. I slip the baggy black t-shirt over my head, and it stops at my mid-thigh. I dry my hair as I stroll back to the kitchen, feeling exposed in nothing but a t-shirt. Rik is going through the first aid kit on the counter, and he glances up at me as I walk back into the kitchen.

"Get on the counter," he instructs.

I do so nervously, pulling at the length of my t-shirt. I feel his hand on my thigh, which causes me to cringe away as bad memories surface. His eyes meet mine in understanding as he pulls his hand back peacefully.

"I'm sorry. I am not him, though," he says, referring to Abe. "I am not going to hurt you. I promise." His voice is gentle and reassuring, which calms me.

He gently places his hand back on my leg, sending warm tingles through my body as he examines the wound, causing me to catch my breath. The warmth from his gentle touch against my skin makes me a little lightheaded.

"Hmm, that's strange," I hear him mumble as he glances up at me. "It's worse than what I thought, but it looks like it has already started healing."

Shit, I forgot about how quickly I heal.

"But you are going to hate what I have to do next," he tells me. I tense up as he reaches for the wound cleaner and a gauze. "We have to disinfect it, and it's probably going to sting like hell," he explains as he opens the bottle.

I nod in understanding as I watch him tilt the bottle over my wound, liquid pouring out. I hiss in pain as it meets the injury. Seeing my pained expression, he gives me an apologetic look.

After torturing me with the disinfected, he places a bandage over the wound, securing it gently in place. Then, he carefully helps me off the counter. I start to feel a little faint; I hear him talking, but I can't quite latch onto anything he says. The feeling turns quickly to being lightheaded, almost like I am on a spinning merry-go-round.

"Rik," I breathe. His eyes meet mine with an expression of worry masking his face. "I don't feel so good." I can barely get the words out as I fight to keep my eyes open. I feel unsteady on my feet just as he reaches for me through the haze.

My knees buckle as the darkness takes over.

CHAPTER 15
Alarik's POV

"Rik," she says, her voice slurred and weak, "I don't feel so good."

Looking back at her, I notice that her pale skin looks even paler, her eyes fighting to stay open as she fights the unseen weight pulling them shut. Her eyes finally close, and her legs give out beneath her. I close the short distance as she falls, barely catching her, keeping her from hitting the floor. My heart is pounding hard in my chest as I stare down at the motionless woman in my arms.

"Selen, Selen!" I repeat her name, hoping for a response, but her limp body just dangles in my grasp. I press my pointer and middle finger to the side of her neck, just below her chin; when I feel the steady beat of her heart, a wave of relief flows through my body. My eyes are glued to her as I watch her chest rise and fall beneath my oversized black t-shirt. Her dark hair strays loose from its braid as it flows like a waterfall over my arm.

Violet S.R. Cox

Stop it, damn it, I mentally scold myself as I admire this beautiful broken woman in my arms. Worried by how pale she looks, I am tempted to rush her to the emergency room, but she has already made her wishes clear: no hospitals.

Scooping up her small, slender figure, I am mindful of her injured leg as I walk to her bedroom. I can't help but keep glancing down at her. Walking through the door, I stroll over to the king-size bed and gently place her on the mattress; the shirt rides up her right thigh, revealing a part of a tattoo. It looks like the beginning of a white feather with a light black lining defining detail. Fighting the curious urge to move the shirt up just enough to reveal the rest of the tattoo, I pull the covers over her.

I stand there, staring at her still form. Consumed with worry, not wanting to leave her alone until I know she is okay. I sit on the floor next to the bed, getting lost in my thoughts.

I don't think I've ever reacted so fast before. And I can't believe I thought she had her period when I saw the blood—with how much blood was covering her jeans, I should've known it wasn't. What was I thinking? This wasn't the movie *Carrie*.

By the time we got home, she had stopped bleeding, and the wound looked like it was already healing. I healed fast, but not nearly as quickly as her. There was something different about her... I just can't wrap my head around it. It wasn't just the healing but the way she affected me.

It's the way my name sounds rolling off her tongue, almost hypnotizing, causing me to catch my breath. Seeing her walking out in my black shirt earlier, I realized I had never seen someone look so beautiful in just a t-shirt. I nearly lost control of my breathing just at the sight of her. I feel something lurking beneath that I haven't felt in a long time, not since Grace. But here she was, waking up that part of me again.

The sound of her stirring draws me back to reality as she slowly sits up in bed. Looking around, dazed and confused, her eyes land on me. Surprise floods her face. Standing up from the floor, I sit on the foot of the bed.

"What happened?" she asks.

"You passed out," I tell her. "I'm thinking it was from blood loss."

Color slowly returns to her face as a blush creeps into her cheeks, making her look even cuter. I'm forced to catch my breath at the sight of her.

Would you stop it?

"How are you feeling?" I ask, pushing the thoughts out of my head.

"I feel a little bit better, but definitely embarrassed that I keep passing out. I'm sorry," she says, her voice as soft as velvet.

I watch her unbraid the rest of her hair; it slips loose from its hold as it falls around her in loose waves. I want to pull her close and bury my face into her hair, curious about how it smells. My eyes land on her soft lips, wondering what they taste and feel like against mine.

Fuck, stop it. Stop thinking like this, I internally reprimand myself as I look at the wall behind her, trying to find an excuse to get out of her presence.

"It's okay. Why don't you try to get some more rest? Let your body finish healing, and I'll make something to eat," I suggest as I stand up off the bed.

    I hurriedly leave the room, shutting the door behind me and taking a deep breath as I walk to the kitchen. Being around her is intoxicating, and I can't think straight.

    I walk into the kitchen, pissed off for breaking the promise I made to myself years ago. After Grace committed suicide, it tore me apart, and I never wanted to get close to anyone for fear of losing them like I lost Grace and my mom.

    Even though I promised myself I would never get attached again, here I was, falling for Selen.

Chapter 16

I watch as Rik leaves the room in a hurry, almost as if to escape me. I get a sense that I have done something. Pushing myself off the bed and walking to the kitchen, I find him cooking in front of the stove. He glances up at me as I walk to the breakfast bar before returning his attention back to the food.

"Did I do something to upset you?" I question him, getting the vibe that he doesn't want to be near me, almost as if he is returning to the cold front he put on for show.

He glances over at me, confusion written on his face.

"You practically ran out of the room," I say, pointing back toward my door.

"No, you didn't do anything to upset me. I just thought you could use rest and maybe eat something," he says, but I sense there is more to it than that. "And speaking of, didn't I tell you to get some rest?" he adds almost sternly.

"Yeah, I suck at taking demands," I comment as I brace my elbow on the countertop separating us.

"You need to heal." His reply sounds unattached.

"I heal fast. I'm all good to go," I say, watching him add spaghetti noodles to boiling water.

He looks up, shaking his head at me. "There is no way to heal that quick. Not with a wound that bad, especially not in a couple of hours."

"Don't believe me?" I ask, walking around to the other side of the breakfast bar. I jump up on the countertop and motion toward my thigh. "Look for yourself." I move the edge of the shirt, exposing more of my thigh to him, that's sporting an ugly bandage.

Walking over to me, he gently peels the bandage away from my skin; his brief touch sends warmth through my body. Catching my breath, I watch as his eyes meet mine in disbelief at finding the gash gone. Without looking down, I know there is no sign of my skin ever being damaged.

"What are you?" he asks as he places the worn bandage on the counter. He studies me, waiting for an answer before he adds, "No one heals that fast."

I take a deep breath as I look at the ground, trying to figure out what to tell him.

"You aren't going to believe me if I tell you the truth," I say, meeting his eyes nervously.

"Try me."

"Keep an open mind." I focus on my hands, fidgeting with my fingers, as I take a deep breath and swallow past the lump in my throat.

He stands there, waiting patiently for me to speak.

"Remember when I told you that Abe left me to die?" I ask, glancing up at him. He nods in answer, though he's still confused. "Well, the truth is, I *did* die that night. I was bleeding internally from the abuse."

"If you died, then how are you here?" he asks, sounding almost as if he thinks I am crazy.

"I was brought back to life by an immortal."

"Okay, you can stop joking now," he tells me sternly, turning back toward the stove. "If you were turned, that would make you an immortal, too. And they don't exist."

"I'm not joking," I state, my voice stern, which causes him to face me again. "Think about it, Rik. Put the pieces together." I point toward my head. "I had a badly sprained ankle. And let's not forget the time Abe choked me; I should have had bruises around my neck. We both know it should have taken a few days to heal and for the bruises to fade." My eyes are fixed on him as he shrugs it off like nothing is out of the ordinary.

"How about when I broke your arm and threw a blade at you? Which hit you in the thigh. When you woke up, you were healed," I continue. "A broken bone would have taken a few weeks, but it healed within a matter of seconds. The wound on your thigh would have stopped bleeding but wouldn't have healed that quickly on its own. That is because I can also heal people."

He observes me skeptically, unsure if I've had some psychotic break. "Okay, calm down," Rik says, moving his hands in a calming gesture.

"How about the gash from today's practice? You saw it healing right before your eyes."

He just keeps staring, obviously unconvinced. I sigh in aggravation as I glance around the kitchen, my eyes landing on the knife set sitting neatly on the countertop. Shaking my head, I meet his gaze.

"I can prove it," I tell him as I grab one of the knives by the handle, pulling it from its home. His eyes light up with the alarm, and he immediately steps back. I wince as I drag the sharp edge across the palm of my left hand; blood wells up from the fresh cut.

"Selen!" Rik shouts as he rushes to me, worry in his eyes. He grabs the knife from my hand, tossing it on the counter, and grabs me by my arm, trying to pull me toward the sink.

"NO!" I shout, pulling back. He looks up into my eyes. "Watch," I tell him, gesturing with my eyes at my hand.

Sighing and rolling his eyes, he does as I ask. As my skin starts to mend itself back together, I hear a soft gasp escape his lips as he looks up at me in disbelief.

Sweet Vengeance

I feel the tears welling up. "I... I never asked to die," I choke out as I pull my freshly healed hand out of his. I take a deep breath calming myself; I watch as he opens, then closes his mouth as he tries to form words.

"I... need a moment to process this," he says, sounding numb as he turns and walks out of the kitchen.

I look around at the enormous empty kitchen, sighing as I turn, returning to my room. I change into my clothes, laying his shirt on the bed before grabbing my duffle and heading back toward the kitchen door. Knowing it was too much for him, I figured I would leave.

"Selen," I hear his voice call from behind me; not looking back, I reach for the doorknob and hear the footsteps approaching.

"Please, don't leave," he begs behind me, making me catch my breath.

He softly grabs my shoulder, slowly turning me to face him. Avoiding his eyes, I let my hair fall into my face, hiding me from view. Reaching out his hand, he carefully tucks my hair behind my ear. He gently grabs my chin between his pointing finger and thumb, tilting my chin up so I can stare into his gorgeous, stormy-blue eyes.

"I don't want you to leave."

I feel my breath hitch.

"I can't keep up this charade anymore. I am so tired of pretending and lying," I admit, my eyes glued to his. I see a mix of emotions flash through them. My heart pounds loudly in my chest, and my throat feels like it is closing up as he looks at me, confused.

"What are you talking about?" he asks as his thumb strokes my cheek, making breathing almost impossible. I close my eyes as his touch leaves a trail of warmth.

Grabbing the duffle, he slides it off my shoulder and gently sits it on the floor. "Explain it to me," he softly encourages me.

I open my eyes, looking into his nervously.

"Besides the guy who brought me back to life, you are the only other person I feel like I can trust," I admit as I look at him. He is so close that his cologne surrounds me in its earthy coffee-mixed aroma, so close that I can see the bright specks of blue in his eyes. Without thinking, I lean forward; I feel the softness of his lips for a split second before I pull back, shaking my head.

"Oh my god, I am so sorry. I don't know—"

He cuts me off and grabs me by the waist, pulling me close against him as his lips land on mine. His right hand slides up my waist to the back of my neck, and my arms wrap around him as I taste his lips against mine, taking in the flavor of honeysuckle. The world melts away as he deepens the kiss, making me breathless and lightheaded.

We both reluctantly pull away; he leans his forehead against mine, staring into my eyes as a flush creeps into my cheeks.

"Don't apologize," he says breathlessly. "You now see why I don't want you to leave."

Sweet Vengeance

"But, how do you feel about me being an immortal?" I ask him nervously. His thumb strokes my cheek once more as if I was the most fragile thing in the world, and he is afraid of breaking me.

"I started falling in love with you before I knew you were immortal. So it doesn't change how I feel about you," he says.

My heart skips a beat at his words. "Love?" I ask him, surprised.

He smiles, nodding his head. "Yes. Will you please stay?" he asks.

Speechless, I nod my head, smiling.

Violet S.R. Cox

CHAPTER 17
Alarik's POV

After dinner, we retired to the living room to play Left 4 Dead. I sit on the floor leaning against the couch while Selen lay upside down, her legs dangling over the back of the couch with her head by my shoulder. I watch her character run into a wall, realizing she isn't lying about not being much of a gamer. She lets out a small scream as zombies attack her, the controller vibrating in her hands as she grins; I can't believe how beautiful her smile is.

"Are you sure you've done this before?" I jokingly ask as her character runs into another wall.

"It's been a while," she admits, glancing over at me and sticking her tongue out. "So leave me alone." She returns her upside-down attention to the game.

Sweet Vengeance

"Heads up!" she says as a Hunter pounces and pins my character to the ground. Her character shoots it and revives me.

"Not bad," I comment as we continue to the safe house. My mind isn't exactly on the game; it's as if I'm under her spell, and I can't help but keep stealing glances at her. On top of that, I can't stop thinking about the kiss we shared earlier. I can still feel her soft, plump lips against mine, delicate like a flower petal and sweeter than chocolate.

As I watch the beautiful woman next to me, I can't help but lean down, pressing my lips to hers. I hear a muffled gasp of surprise, followed by the sound of her setting the controller on the floor.

Her hands gently grab my neck as her lips move against mine in response. The world seems to melt away, leaving only us as the sweet chocolate taste of her lips and the intoxicating scent of fresh flowers consume me.

The screams of our characters getting killed by zombies bring us back to reality as she pulls back, looking at the television.

"You got us killed," she says, shaking her head with a smile that takes my breath away.

I reach up and tickle her, causing her to squirm and fall off the couch with a yelp. She lands on the floor with a soft thud, parallel to the couch, her head near my leg.

"It was worth it," I reply, hovering over her upside-down face. She looks up with deep, soulful eyes that lure me in. I want her lips against mine again; I crave it like an addict would their drug of choice. I lower myself to her sweet mouth, and her smile crashes onto mine as her arms wrap around my neck.

Violet S.R. Cox

I reluctantly pull back, my eyes meeting her bright green ones.

"I want you to feel comfortable and safe with me," I say. "If things ever get too... *intense*, please make me aware. I don't want you afraid of me." I know the trauma she has been through, and I don't want her to think I am being pushy.

She gradually sits up, mindful of my face hovering over hers as she leans against the couch. I sit cross-legged on the floor, facing her as her eyes meet mine.

"I can't begin to tell you how much that means to me," she says. "I wasn't lying when I told you I trust you." She looks down at her hands, fidgeting with her fingers, her hair partially falling into her face.

"I have never felt this way about someone, and I don't want to lose you. Especially because I was being careless." I scoot closer and push her hair gently behind her ear, revealing her face.

She looks up, smiling despite the tears in her eyes.

"I never thought anyone would be worried about losing me," she whispers. "Thank you for respecting me and being so understanding."

By the look in her distant eyes, I know she is having a flashback. I pull her into my arms, hugging her, trying to comfort her and erase the memories.

Abe is hovering over me as the tearing of fabric floods my ears. Fear and pain rush through me. My hands try to slap his away, but a closer look reveals they aren't mine. I watch in horror as his hand explores her body, sending chills through my spine.

Jerking away from her, I meet her concerned and confused eyes.

"That was… That was very intense," I say, gaining a new understanding of what happened.

"What are you talking about?" she questions.

"You somehow pulled me into your… memory with Abe," I tell her, unsure of what truly just happened.

"Oh my God, I am so sorry. I didn't mean to. I didn't know I could do that," she explains, and I know it's true—I can hear the guilt in her voice.

"Don't be. You are safe now," I reassure her, pulling her against me and stroking her hair. "Together, we will make him pay."

CHAPTER 18

I am sitting on the couch, my head on Rik's shoulder as we cuddle, watching a movie. I feel his lips kiss my forehead as his fingers stroke my hair. I glance up into Rik's chocolate brown eyes—no, they aren't his.

I am face to face with Abe.

The fear slams into me, causing me to jerk back. The living room around me disappears, turning to the dark abandoned road.

"I always get what I want. Remember that Scarlett."

Abe grabs my arm, pulling me back to him as he presses his lips against mine.

"NO!"

Sweet Vengeance

My shouts wake me as I bolt upright in the bed, tears streaming down my face, my heart beating furiously in my chest as I fight to breathe.

Bang. The door slams open, causing me to look up from the bed to find Rik's figure dashing through the dark.

"Selen, are you okay?" he asks as he lands on the bed, pulling me into an embrace, his hand stoking my hair. "It's okay, It's okay. It was just a nightmare. You are safe." He calms me with his whispers, and I shakily look at him.

"I'm—" I stutter, tears streaming down my cheeks. "I'm sorry."

"Don't be," he tells me as I bury my face into his shoulder.

I don't know how long we sit in silence; our breathing is the only sound as he sits there, comforting me, practically holding me in his lap.

After finally calming down, I carefully tilt my head to him, pressing my lips to his. I feel the softness of his lips against mine as he returns the kiss, reassuring me that I am safe.

I pull away, looking at him in the dark.

"You okay?" he asks me as his hand rubs over my back in circles. I nod, afraid to speak. "I'll stay with you until you fall back asleep."

"I'll... I'll be okay," I answer quickly, panicking at the suggestion. "I'm sorry. It's nothing against you. I'm... just not comfortable with us staying in the same bed right now." I rush through the explanation, afraid of angering him.

"Don't be. I understand," he says gently, stroking my hair. "If you need anything, just holler, and I'll be there." He pushes himself off the bed, immediately leaving coldness in his absence.

I watch his figure walk out the door, leaving me alone in the unforgiving darkness. Taking a shaky breath, I lay back down on the bed.

This is all Abe's fault, I think angrily. He ruined my life and has me living in fear; I shouldn't be afraid of being with a guy. I wish I could live my life like an ordinary girl, but…

The fear will always be there.

Chapter 19

The following morning, I crawl out of bed and open the bedroom door, following the soft sound of the television playing in the living room. Rik is lying on the couch, his arm behind his head as he watches whatever is on the TV. He glances up at me as I walk in, pulling himself into a sitting position, and gestures to the spot next to him. Silently, I sit down, still embarrassed from last night.

"Nice pj's," he comments as he studies me, making me blush. "Morning, beautiful. How are you feeling?"

"Morning." I try to think of a way to avoid where this conversation is going. "How about training today?" I ask as I glance away, not wanting to drag him into my demons.

He gently lifts my chin, locking eyes with me. "You don't have to go through this alone. I am here to help."

"I don't want to be a burden," I mutter as my heart compresses and my emotions threaten to overtake me.

"You, Miss Sirus, are not a burden," he says, his voice becoming serious. "Don't ever think that." He strokes my cheek with his thumb, making me catch my breath; my heart skips a beat, and warm tingles spread through my body.

"Okay, can we please train? I deal better when I am distracted," I practically beg him as he stares deeply into my eyes. "Plus, if we are going to take Abe out, we have to learn each other's fighting skills," I add.

"Yes, but only cause you have a point," he says, standing up and extending his hand to help me off the couch. Pulling me close against him, he leans down to kiss me. But suddenly, the nightmare flashes in my brain. I step out of his arms, leaving him staring at me. Hurt flashes through his eyes for a split second before he nods in understanding.

"On your own time, when you are ready," he says, sincerity reflecting deep in his eyes. "I want to help replace those bad memories with new ones and see that beautiful smile on your face more often."

"Thank you," I whisper as I pull my arms close to my body. "I am going to go get changed for training."

I head back to my room, but once I'm there, I feel the guilt weigh on me. Taking a deep breath, I quickly change into black leggings and a crop top. I brush my hair into a ponytail before leaving the room to find Rik, already transformed, waiting for me outside his bedroom door.

"How about we practice in the backyard today?" he asks as he leads the way outside.

"Sounds good to me," I reply as we step out the door.

"Training starts now," he says, spinning toward me. His hand immediately goes to my throat and slams my back against the house. His grip isn't as tight as Abe's, but it's enough to spike the fear within me.

"Don't give into the fear. Turn it into anger," he instructs, studying my reaction. "Damn it, fight!" he shouts, trying to get me to kick into action.

And it works.

The fear slips away as my training kicks in. Bringing my arms up straight in the air and dropping them over his outstretched arm, I break his hold and shove him away.

"That's my girl," he says as he regains his balance. Now, he's blocking the steps off the porch.

"What the fuck was that?" I demand as I creep toward the railing. His gaze tracks my every step as he starts for me again.

"You want to train, let's train," he says. "I'm not going to take it easy on you."

He rapidly closes the distance between us. Leaping over the barrier, I land softly on the grass below and run toward the center of the expansive open yard, trying to keep from getting backed into a corner again. I turn, facing him as he stalks closer to me.

"Fine. But I might hurt you," I tell him, fearing my strength that I don't have complete control of yet.

"You can heal me if you do. But we have to learn each other's weaknesses," he states simply as he swings his fist toward my face.

I barely dodge as the air brushes across my cheek. I block his other fist with my arm, grabbing his arm midair; I bring my knee up into his stomach and quickly sweep my legs out from under him. He lands on the ground with a soft thud and a groan.

"I warned you," I tell him as he stands up, panting.

He sprints toward me. I swing my fist when he's within reach, but he stops suddenly, dodging, and grabs my arm while I am off balance. I stumble into him, sending us both to the ground with me on top. The feel of his body against mine sends electricity down my spine. He rolls on top of me, taking my breath away as I lay sprawled under him, staring up at him. With him so close, my body is on fire.

"Rik," I breathe as I press upward, my lips clashing furiously against his. I feel him stiffen for a moment before he returns the hungry kiss. He has one arm wrapped around my back, his legs on either side of mine, and his hand wrapped into my hair. I lose myself in the kiss and feel his hand go to the edge of my shirt, caressing my side as things heat up—a little too much, stirring familiar discomfort inside me. I pull away from him.

"Rik, I'm sorry," I whisper breathlessly as I mentally push the dark memories away. "Things are getting a little too intense for me." He immediately retracts his hand from my stomach.

"I'm so sorry," he says, immediately pushing himself off of me to sit beside me.

Sweet Vengeance

"Don't be. I kinda instigated it," I say as warmth spreads into my cheeks. "I don't know what it is about you, but I'm so relaxed around you. I feel something that I have never felt before. It's almost like you're breaking down my walls and making me feel again."

"You're doing the same to me," he says, "but like I told you, I will not take advantage of you. I want you to take your time." He reaches out a hand, placing it against the side of my face, his thumb stroking my cheek. "I will wait."

"Thank you," I whisper, my eyes glued to him.

We lay together in silence, the sun bathing us in its bright light. I lean back, soaking in the warmth against my body, simply enjoying each other's company.

I feel hands picking me up, and I open my eyes to see Rik lifting me with a grin as he runs toward the pool and jumps off the edge. The coldness of the water surrounds me as we both go under. Pushing out of his arms, I swim to the surface and come face to face with him; his huge grin greets me as he lets out a laugh.

Splashing water in his face, I take off swimming in the other direction. I hear him swimming after me, then only the sound of my strokes. Suddenly, hands grab me from under the water, dragging me beneath the surface before releasing their hold.

I return to the surface, sputtering and wiping the water off my face; I find Rik a few feet away with a mischievous grin. Slowly swimming to him, I wrap my arms around his neck and press my lips against his. As I break the kiss and pull back, I smile up at him, feeling like a teenager.

"Thank you for everything," I whisper.

"The pleasure was all mine," he whispers back, leaning his forehead against mine.

Rik takes me in his arms, carrying me to the pool's edge and setting me on it. I lay on my back to look up at the sky, and Rik pulls himself out of the pool to join me. I scoot closer to him and lay my head on his chest. It softly rises and falls under my cheek as his arms wrap around my shoulder.

We lay there for a few moments when I finally sit up, stretching.

"I'm going to go change out of these wet clothes," I explain as I push myself off the ground, offering him my hand. He takes it and stands. We both walk toward the house.

"So, um, what are you into?" I ask him, wanting to know more about him.

"You," he says, surprising me. "Sorry."

"Don't be," I reply as we approach the porch.

He opens the door, gestures for me to go first, and then follows me inside.

"How about you go change, and we can watch a movie if you want," he suggests. I nod in answer.

"That sounds great," I tell him as we walk to our separate rooms.

After changing back into my pajamas, I find him in the living room, sitting on the couch, waiting for me. I join him, and he pulls me close as he puts on a shark movie. I curl up beside him as the movie starts and that's how we end the rest of the night.

Chapter 20

  I feel the warmth under my cheek rising and falling. Opening my eyes, I find the back of the couch. Glancing up, I see Rik asleep, looking so peaceful and at ease, with his arm loosely wrapped around me to keep me from falling off the couch. I try to slowly sit up without waking him, but the slight movement causes him to bolt upright; with a yelp, I fall to the floor. He glances around, dazed, until he realizes what happened.

  "Shit, Selen. I am so sorry. I didn't mean to fall asleep with you," he apologizes as he quickly stands, helping me off the floor.

  "It's okay."

  "No, it's not. I just betrayed your trust."

  "Rik," I say his name, cutting him off as we take our seats back on the couch. "It's okay, I'm not upset. That is the first time I actually got a full night's sleep." As I finish my explanation, a look of surprise passes over his features.

Violet S.R. Cox

"But I should have made—"

I press my lips against his, silencing him. Pulling back, I press our foreheads together.

"Shut up. I'm saying that I actually enjoyed it," I tell him. "So please stop blaming yourself." He nods in agreement as I get up.

"Where are you going?" he asks curiously.

"To make breakfast," I say as I walk into the kitchen.

From my place at the stove, I feel the warmth of his arms as they gently wrap around my waist, followed by the press of his body against mine and the soft brush of his lips against my cheek, all before I finish making the scrambled eggs.

Turning the stove off, he gently turns me around in his arms with a breathtaking smile. Leaning down, he gingerly presses his lips against mine as I wrap my arms around his neck, returning the kiss hungrily. The world seems to melt away, leaving just the two of us. The kisses become more profound, more intense, and more passionate. His tongue sneaks past my lips, teasing mine, driving me into a frenzy.

A fire sparks deep in my stomach as I move against him, the pressure building in my groin—something I have never felt before—as my body aches to be satisfied. He pushes me until my back is against the counter, pressing his body against mine lustfully. My hand plays with his short ponytail at the base of his neck as our tongues dance together. I feel him lift me up onto the countertop by my thighs, his touch sending sparks flying through my body, igniting a new need.

Sweet Vengeance

He pulls back, resting his forehead against mine as we both pant breathlessly, and his eyes shine with newfound lust as he stares at me. Every fiber in my being wants and needs him. I wrap my legs around his waist, pulling him closer as my lips return eagerly to his when he suddenly breaks the kiss and pulls away; I look at him, confused.

Did I do something wrong?

"I don't think this is a good idea. Things are getting heated, and I don't want to lose control," he says as he runs his hand nervously through his braided hair, though the spark of desire lingers in his eyes. I know he is trying to keep me from getting hurt, but that doesn't mean the rejection didn't sting.

I want you, though.

"Oh, that's fine," I say, trying to hide the hurt within me as I hop off the counter. "I was actually planning on taking a shower anyway."

"It's not like that. I just don't want it to be a mistake," he tries to explain, but the word *mistake* knocks my breath out of me like I just got punched in the gut.

Mistake? Does that mean he thinks I'm a mistake? I feel the hurt turn to anger as I meet his eyes.

"For who?" I snarl at him. "If I didn't want anything to happen, I would have stopped you." I storm off, filled with disappointment, fighting against the tears threatening to escape as I internally scold myself for being so foolish.

Stupid. You threw yourself at him like a dog in heat.

Violet S.R. Cox

I close the bedroom door behind me as the first tear slides down my cheek. Angrily wiping it away, I walk into the bathroom and turn the shower on. Slipping out of my clothing, I step into the warm spray of the shower and let the tears flow freely with the water down the drain.

Standing beneath the hot water, I feel the self-pity washing away.

Chapter 21
Alarik's POV

She's driving me crazy. Selen's legs are wrapped around my waist, pulling me closer as her addicting lips land on mine again, the kiss heating up. As much as I want to give in to the lust that threatens to overtake me, I don't want to take advantage of her and pressure her into something she might not be ready for. If I did, what would make me better than Abe?

I reluctantly pull away from her, trying to think clearly, which is impossible in our current position. As soon as I pull away from her, I immediately regret it when I see the confusion and hurt in her bright green eyes.

"I don't think this is a good idea. Things are getting heated, and I don't want to lose control."

"Oh, that's fine. I was actually planning on taking a shower anyway," she tells me, trying to play it off as she hops off the counter.

"It's not like that. I just don't want it to be a mistake," I try to explain, but the look in her eyes tells me I picked the wrong word. I mentally slap myself for not choosing my words more carefully.

"For who?" she questions with profound hurt in her voice. "If I didn't want anything to happen, I would have stopped you."

She walks out of the kitchen, leaving me silently cursing myself as I watch her go.

What the fuck was I thinking? She was correct; if she didn't want it to go any further, she would have stopped me, as she has done before. I should have read the signs—this time, she was pressing for more, and I didn't catch on to the signals.

Unsure if I should follow or give her her space, I stand there weighing the pros and cons before finally deciding to walk down the hall to her room. Stopping outside her closed bedroom door, I hear the faint sound of water running. Sighing, I walk to the living room and wait in the recliner, zoning out as I replay the kiss with different scenarios.

I hear the shower finally cut off, pulling me away from my thoughts. Taking a nervous breath, I stand and return to her door, gently rapping my knuckles against the solid wood.

Please give me another chance.

"Please go away." Her voice is muffled through the door, but she sounds depressed. I think carefully about what to say next.

Sweet Vengeance

"Did you really just restrict me from a room in my own house?" I ask, my voice amused and teasing as I lean against the door frame, waiting for a reply. I hear her sigh, and soft footsteps come toward me. The handle turns, and the door creaks open.

"What?" she asks, revealing nothing but a red towel wrapped around her body as she dries her long hair with another, her eyes a little red and puffy from crying.

Pretend like you don't notice and make her forget the hurt.

My eyes travel the length of her perfect body, hiding beneath the thin fabric, jealous of the towel as it touches her bare skin. I feel my member pulsating in excitement.

How can someone be sexy in nothing but a towel?

I see her lips moving but can't hear her over my racing heartbeat. Closing the distance between us, I cup her face in my hands, startling her; she drops the towel she was drying her hair with as I anxiously press my lips against her perfectly plump ones. Her mouth moves against mine before she pulls back, looking up at me confused.

"Are you sure you're ready?" I whisper, leaning my forehead against hers, searching her eyes for any doubt, but all I see is lust and hope. Biting her bottom lip, which makes me want her that much more, she nervously nods.

"I want to hear you say it," I tell her softly, her eyes full of longing and need.

"Yes. More than you know," she breathes against my lips. "But do you want—"

I cut her off as my lips clash with hers in a frenzy, greedily devouring her taste. My hands wrap around her waist, slowly guiding her backwards to the bed without breaking the kiss. The back of her knees hit the edge of the mattress; slowly lowering her onto the bed, I straddle either side of her legs.

My tongue slips past her parted lips, teasing her playfully, sending sparks through me. I lower my lips to her jawline, slowly making my way down. She catches her breath as I leave kisses on her collarbone. I can hear her heart beating rapidly; glancing up, a noticeable flush is creeping into her cheeks.

I carefully pull my shirt over my head and let it drop to the floor. My eyes meet hers, silently asking permission before continuing—she nods yes. Her eyes are glued to mine as I reach out and slowly remove the towel from her body; I keep glancing up to make sure she doesn't change her mind or feel uncomfortable. As I admire her perfect curves that the towel was hiding, I stop to catch my breath. It should be illegal for someone to look this good in nothing.

Now, I'm finally able to see the whole tattoo on her thigh; it starts at her hip bone and is about the size of my hand. I was right about it being a feather, but there are two: one black with a white spot and one white with a black spot. The way the feathers are positioned reminds me of the yin and yang symbol.

Tearing my eyes away from the tattoo, I return my attention to the naked woman lying on the bed before me.

I furiously kiss her lips, my hand grabbing her bare hip as she shakily sucks in a breath between core-rattling kisses. My hand gradually moves up her body as I explore her every curve, her skin as smooth as velvet beneath my touch.

Sweet Vengeance

My other hand rests on the back of her neck; one of her hands is wrapped in my hair, and the other is on my chest, exploring, leaving electricity in its wake.

I gingerly kiss my way to her jawline and neck and gently bite down, causing her to groan softly as the pleasure builds within her. Her breathing hitches with every kiss until my mouth reaches her perfectly round breast.

I glance up at her, meeting her gaze to see the excitement and nervousness shining in those beautiful green eyes. I gently take her hard, perky nipple in my mouth; a soft moan escapes her lips as I circle her sensitive nipple with the tip of my tongue. I rub her other breast, gently pinching her other nipple. Her soft moans of bliss fill the room, making me even harder as I try to concentrate on keeping the pace slow, making this night all about her.

But *damn*, she's making it very difficult not to take her in this very moment.

Chapter 22

The tip of Rik's tongue circles my over-sensitive nipple, sending bursts of bliss through me. His hands explore my body, his touch as soft as a feather caressing my skin; it's enough to drive me into an unspeakable frenzy as I crave something I never realized my body desperately wanted. My heart races with excitement and anticipation as his hand travels the length of my hip, the proximity making my groin pulsate with eagerness, wetness already building between my legs.

Rik's mouth brushes against the bottom of my breast as he slowly goes lower, leaving a trail of kisses in his wake, sending warm tremors throughout me until he stops at my intimate spot. He gently parts my thighs, rubbing the inside, when he leans down, snaking his tongue over my clit.

I catch my breath at the intense pleasure that floods me. He furiously flicks his tongue over all the right spots, sending my body into spasms as I squirm and grab the bed sheets. I bite my lower lip, trying to suppress the moans threatening to escape my lips.

Sweet Vengeance

One of his hands sneaks up to my breast, cupping it, and gently squeezes my nipple between his fingers, which only adds to the blazing fire in me as he sucks on my throbbing clit.

I let out a soft moan as he hungrily eats me out, the pressure building in the pit of my stomach as another spasm racks my body. I feel his mouth leave me; glancing down, I watch as he wipes his mouth with the back of his hand and stands up. Rik unbuttons his pants, slipping them off, followed by his boxers. I notice his thick shaft standing at attention as I let my eyes travel the length of his body, catching my breath as I admire his well-toned body, only stopping when I meet his stormy blue eyes.

I scoot myself further up until my head is on the pillow and anxiously await his return. He eases onto the bed, crawling to me, and gently spreads my legs, carefully positioning himself between them. His eyes lock on mine, almost as if seeing into my soul.

"Are you sure?" he asks me one last time, giving me a chance to back out.

"Yes," I whisper, breathless.

With those words, his lips land on mine hungrily as he reaches between my legs, his fingers stroking my wet lips. He eases one finger in, causing me to catch my breath with the sudden but brief discomfort, followed by a second finger, eliciting a muffled moan against his mouth.

"That's my girl," he whispers against my lips as he slides his finger in and out of me, sending me into a frenzy of pure desire.

I need more.

I'm on the verge of exploding as another tremble racks my body. He removes his fingers, grabbing his length and positioning himself at my entrance.

Breaking the kiss, we lock eyes as he eases into me. A brief but welcomed pain leaves me gasping. He stops, his gaze searching mine.

"Are you hurt?" he asks out of concern; I shake my head no.

He leans forward, kissing me as he slowly moves his hips, turning the brief pain into pleasure. He thrusts soft and slow, letting me get used to the size of him. Wrapping my legs around him, I feel him slip deeper inside me, causing me to moan in pleasure.

I never thought it would feel this good.

As his movements quicken, the pressure builds, throbbing its way through my body. Digging my nails hard into his back, waves of pleasure flood my body; my hips move against his, the motion subconscious as I meet his thrust halfway.

The sounds of my moans fall around us as he speeds up. He growls low as he grabs my hips, pushing deeper inside me. Time ceases to exist as we grind against each other, losing ourselves to the lust as our bodies furiously clash against each other, leaving us panting. His strokes get harder and faster; suppressing a scream, I bite my lower lip.

"Don't do that," he tells me, breathless, as he pushes deeper inside. "I want to hear you."

As he leans back, grabbing my thighs, he slams into me, putting me on the verge of screaming. I feel him swelling inside me with each spasm passing through my body, causing me to cry out.

Sweet Vengeance

"Rik!" I moan his name loudly, grabbing the pillows and sheets as I arch my back. I am on the verge of exploding as he somehow goes deeper—his hard cock, buried within me, pulses as he nears his climax.

With a scream, the earth-shattering orgasm explodes within me; with one last thrust, a moan escapes past his lips as he gets his sweet release.

I shake beneath him as he braces himself on his elbows, still inside me.

"Are you okay?" he asks me breathlessly. His eyes stare into mine as he strokes my cheek softly. "I didn't hurt you, did I?"

"No, that was amazing," I say, panting as I lay there, naked and sweaty.

He carefully pulls out of me, which makes my breath hitch, before he lays down next to me and pulls my naked body close.

"That it was," he whispers against my neck as we cuddle.

My eyes start to get heavy as the adrenaline leaves my body. I am almost asleep in his arms when I feel him sit up, startling me.

"Shit. Fuck, fuck!" he curses, jumping out of bed.

I wrap the sheet around my naked body, confused, watching as he starts pacing the floor.

"What?" I ask, feeling the panic seeping in. "Rik, what's wrong?"

He stops, his eyes reflecting panic as they meet mine.

Please don't say you regret it.

"I am so sorry. I royally fucked up," he begins, nervously running a hand through his hair. "I didn't use protection. God, I can't believe I forgot to use a condom. Damn it, I am sorry Selen."

I feel my body relax as I realize what he is thinking. "It's alright—"

"No, it's not okay. I may have just gotten you pregnant." He raises his voice, causing me to flinch. He notices and immediately looks guilty. "I'm sorry. I just feel awful for screwing up."

"If you would shut up for one second and let me explain something," I tell him as I stand up. Suddenly self-conscious about being naked in front of him, I take the sheet with me.

He looks at me, puzzled, as I go to sit at the foot of the bed. "Being immortal has some perks. One of them happens to be a kind of built-in birth control." I look at the ground shyly as I explain. "I can choose when or if I want to have kids," I tell him, almost absent-minded.

"Oh," he says, taking a seat beside me. "Now I feel kind of stupid for freaking out like that. Sorry."

"It's not your fault," I say, shrugging. "I should have told you, but I didn't think about it in the heat of the moment."

Rik climbs back under the covers and gestures for me to join him. We both lay down, and he pulls me against his perfectly naked body, gently caressing my side and hip.

Sweet Vengeance

"You are amazing," he whispers against the back of my neck. I feel a smile forming on my lips.

"So," he starts awkwardly, causing me to glance back at him. "This is the tattoo I supposedly paid for years ago?" he asks, tracing his finger over the feather tattoo on my hip and leaving trails of heat in their wake.

Confused, I look up at him. "What are you talking about?"

"The night I saved you," he says. "When you lied to get under Abe's skin. You told him that I paid for it," he explains, refreshing my mind.

"Oh. Yeah," I reply, giggling as I recall the look on Abe's face.

"What does it mean? If you don't mind me asking."

"Of course. The feathers are meant to remind me that freedom is close, that all I have to do is spread my wings. The black and white represents yin and yang, which reminds me that bad things can happen to good people; there can never be a positive without a negative. You put those meanings together, and—"

"It means, no matter the darkness, you are still fighting. You're going to find a way to get out because even the darkest moments have a light at the end," he finishes.

I nod my head, smiling.

"Well, I think that's maybe the best imagery money I ever spent," he adds, making me chuckle as I cuddle against him.

He pulls the covers over us as I succumb to the darkness of sleep in his warm arms.

Abe is in the driver's seat in the dark car, his hand on my thigh moving in small circles. I push his hand away softly.

"I'm sorry, Abe, I'm not ready," I explain, but from the look in his eyes, I can tell he isn't happy about the rejection.

His hand clamps on the back of my neck, pulling me closer. Our faces only inches apart, he forces his lips onto mine before traveling to my neck; he sucks and nibbles my soft flesh. He starts groping me, but I'm shoving his hands away, struggling to escape his touch.

"No!" I sternly tell him, my back against the car door.

"I always get what I want," he says. "You're better off just giving in. That way, you don't get hurt."

Abe reaches for me again. I extend my hand behind me, searching blindly for the handle. After finding it, I open the door and bolt out of the car.

"Scarlett! Come back here!" I hear Abe call as I dart down the dark road.

The panic and fear seep into my body as I hear his heavy footsteps behind me.

But suddenly, Alarik appears out of nowhere, grabs me, and brings me into the darkness of the woods. He pulls me into a hug; the pitch-black woods turn bright, and Abe is gone.

Sweet Vengeance

I feel safe.

Looking up at Rik, his lips meet mine, and the taste of honeysuckle comforts me.

CHAPTER 23

I wake to Rik's warm body against mine, his arm draped over my waist and his face buried in my hair at the base of my neck. His soft breathing warmly caresses my skin, sending goosebumps across my body. I slowly peel myself away from him, trying not to wake him. But when I move his arm, he starts to stir. I slowly stand up from the bed, glancing back at him; he's awake and admiring my body.

"Where you going?" he questions as I grab the towel off the floor, self-consciously wrapping it around my naked body and walking toward the bathroom.

"I need a shower. Did you want to join?" I turn to ask him seductively; he raises his eyebrows, intrigued, as he stands from the bed, completely naked. My eyes roam his body, taking in every muscle and perfect curve.

Realizing that I'm staring, I look everywhere but at him, trying to avoid the voice in my head telling me to press my body against his again. I hear a soft chuckle, then footsteps coming to me as he pulls me into his arms.

Sweet Vengeance

"Why don't we use the shower in my bathroom? It's better than this one," he says, his finger stroking the center of my bare back. A warm tingling flows through me as I tilt my head back, sighing, my knees threatening to buckle.

"Sure," I whisper, curious about how his bedroom looks. "Lead the way."

As he pulls his hand away, I'm suddenly brought back to my senses. Rik passes through the doorway, and I follow his naked body diagonally across the hall to his door.

The bedroom that lies behind it is enormous. I walk in slowly, my eyes taking in the glossy black walls that meet white trim on a black wooden floor that spreads throughout the room. A huge, king-size black platform bed sits against the far wall. The two dressers match the bed, adorned with silver handles. A burgundy red comforter set is the only splash of color in the whole room, besides a random book sitting on his nightstand and a few articles of clothing thrown around.

A painting above one of the dressers captures my attention; curiously, I walk over and stop in front of it.

"I didn't know you were into art," I comment, admiring the painting of a skeleton in the motion of standing up, fire surrounding it as if rising from the ashes, ready to fight. A thin mask of white covers the whole painting, giving it a smoky look. Next to the skeleton, I see the small white signature of the artist: *SSS*.

"Oh, yeah. But mostly just this artist," he says, coming up beside me to admire the painting. "They are amazing at what they do. I wish I could get more, but they cost around ten grand each and sell out pretty quickly."

"I've heard of the artist. Apparently, no one knows who it is," I say, recalling what I'd heard. "Whoever they are, I love how they painted this one. It can be taken in so many ways. One that comes to mind is the skeleton battling a... um, demon, or fear, and rising out of it. Overcoming it. Preparing themselves for war," I try my best to explain. He watches me, amused at my thoughts.

"I can see that. I thought they were coming out of war and trying to regain their mindset. You know, like how Marines return to civilian life, trying to readjust from war to civilization," he explains before taking my hand in his and leading me to the bathroom.

Walking through the door, I find myself in a dark bathroom. The deep gray paint on the walls extends about halfway down until it meets white beadboard, ending at a gray tiled floor, speckled black. Off to the left stands a black double-sink vanity that runs about half the wall. A mirror of the same length is placed above it, emphasized with shiny black trim to match.

Across from the vanity lies the vast shower, with double shower heads on either side and one suspended from the ceiling to give the rain effect. The gray and black tiles on the shower floor meet the solid black tiles on the wall, with a four-shelf built in to hold shower supplies. The glass door goes all the way to the ceiling. To the side of the massive shower, Rik is messing with a silver panel; when the red numbers pop up, I realize it's one of those showers where you can adjust the temperature of the water.

On the other side of the shower is the most oversized black Jacuzzi tub with a stainless steel silver faucet, and the tile matching the floor encases the edges. In the corner, away from the tub, is a black toilet. Black bath mats lay in front of the bathtub, shower, and vanity.

I hear the sound of running water, returning my attention to the perfectly naked Rik standing before me.

Sweet Vengeance

"You joining me?" he asks as he steps into the shower.

I walk the short distance and self-consciously peel the towel away from my body. My cheeks heat up as I hang it on the hook beside the shower, exposing myself as I step inside. The hot water causes me to gasp from the sudden temperature change. But as it pounds against my skin, I lean into it, letting the water massage away the soreness from last night.

I feel hands on my shoulder, Rik's electric touch setting my body ablaze as his hands slowly make their way down my arms. Fingers creep across my wet stomach, and my breath hitches at the contact as I lean back into him, the hot water raining down on my breasts and abdomen adding to the tingling sensation in my skin.

"You up for shower sex?" he whispers into my ear, the warmth in my belly building. I nod my head as the need and want seep into me.

"Yes," I whisper anxiously.

Rik's hand travels lower, gently stroking my begging lips; with his other hand, he moves my long, wet hair over my shoulder and leans down, pressing his lips to my neck. I feel the warm, pulsating tingle as I gasp in excitement. I lean back into him as if becoming one with him, as he gently sneaks two fingers into me, teasing me.

A rush of excitement courses through my body when I feel his hard erection pressing against my bare back. I can't help but let out a series of soft moans as he plunges his finger in and out of my drenched entrance, eager for more attention.

Violet S.R. Cox

Finally, he pulls them out, carefully turning me to face him; his eyes admire me hungrily. His lips land lustfully against mine, devouring my taste as our mouths clash. His hands slide down to my waist, pulling me closer to him. Our naked, soaking-wet bodies press against each other fearlessly as our desire overtakes us, making the world fade away.

He moves me, my back pressing against the shower wall, and grabs my hips to lift me up. We lock eyes, and the need in his gaze is overpowering. Pulling back, he balances my weight in one hand, positioning himself at my entrance, and he pushes himself inside me.

He slips in and out with ease, grabbing my hips as he moves. I arch my back, throwing back my head as the bliss of each thrust racks my body into a frenzy, my nerves blazing and hungry for more. As if he knows what I want, I hear his breath hitch before slamming his entire length into me. My body is at his complete mercy as he pounds harder, each thrust bringing me to the brink of screaming. I wrap my arms around him, my nails digging into his back as I suppress a moan; I bite down on his shoulder as another earth-shattering wave of pleasure floods my body, leaving my toes curled and legs trembling.

"Rik," I moan, looking into his eyes; they glisten with a determination I have never seen. "I don't know how much longer I can last."

"Not yet. Hold on just a little longer," he says as he furiously pounds deep inside me, bringing me even closer to the edge. I know he must be close, too, and I feel him growing inside me as he nears his climax.

With one last, deep thrust, he pulses inside me as he orgasms; it's enough to send me into my own unforgiving release, ripping a scream of pleasure from deep within me.

Sweet Vengeance

In the end, we're both left gasping for breath.

He pulls his length out of me, setting me on my feet; my legs are like jelly beneath me, forcing me to hold onto the shower wall for support.

"Wow," I whisper as I regain control of my breathing and muscles.

Rik is under the spray of the shower, still eyeing me hungrily.

How much more does he want?

Chapter 24
Alarik's POV

I swear I have a slight addiction to her; I can't keep my hands off her. I mean, I could, but why would I? I didn't want to get out of the shower, especially with her amazingly wet naked body sandwiched between me and the wall. The honeysuckle taste lingers on my lips, and I'm hungry for more.

I watch Selen dry herself off before wrapping the towel around her slender body. Her bright green eyes remind me of lily pads, while her dark hair contrasts with her fair skin tone, making her look even more perfect. Her scars make her stunning, and her strong willpower is breathtaking.

I don't understand how anyone could ever hurt her or would want to. Why hurt this beautiful broken creature who is still standing and fighting instead of giving in to the depression? You would never know that she had gone through hell and back with how she carries herself. Besides having nightmares, she was coping pretty well. After getting that flashback, I am surprised to see how well she is managing, considering everything.

Sweet Vengeance

"Do you think you could give me a ride home? I need to grab a few things," she asks, her voice soft as satin. I watch as she pulls herself onto the vanity counter between the double sinks.

Oh, she's at the perfect height. How good would it feel in that position? No, stop thinking with your other head.

My eyes travel her body, stopping on her eyes.

"Yeah, of course," I answer, trying to keep my imagination at bay as it plays out all the different ways I could make her squirm and scream on that counter.

"Thank you." She hops off the counter and heads for the door.

"Who said you could leave with that towel on?" I ask, disappointed that her body is hidden beneath it.

She stops at the door, glancing back at me with a smile plastered on her face. "Oh, that's right. You can keep the towel," she says as she lets the towel slip from her breathtaking, goddess-like body, revealing her perfectly round ass and supple curves. Her dark, damp hair stops at her mid-back, leaving droplets trailing across her flawless skin.

Selen puts her hands on either side of the door, glancing back at me with a smirk, and I swear I can see a twinkle of seduction in her green eyes; the confidence surrounding her shines as she stands naked in front of me.

"I'm going to go get dressed," she says as she walks through the door, leaving me with another boner.

Violet S.R. Cox

I groan in torment as I fight the urge to follow her, throw her on the bed, and fuck her into another world. *Why does she make me feel this way? The constant need and want?* Whatever this is, it is incredible.

Selen is the perfect addiction.

After getting dressed, I walking out of my bedroom to find her sitting on the second step of the stairs, pulling her shoes on. She's wearing a red tank top that clings to her like a second skin and black skinny jeans to perfectly show off her hips. Her healthy long hair cascades behind her shoulders.

She looks up, catching me staring as I take in every one of her features. Her plump, tender, tasty lips were the correct shade of pink on her.

I wonder how those lips would feel somewhere else. Rik. Stop. It. Show a little respect.

"Ready?" I ask, trying to get my mind out of the gutter.

She bends down, grabbing the duffle on the floor before standing. "When you are," she says, slinging the bag over her shoulder.

I step toward her and take the duffle from her, gesturing in front of me.

"Let's go," I reply as she leads the way out of the door and to my car, which sits in the graveled driveway.

I pick up my pace, getting ahead to open the car door for her, and once she is in, I gently shut it. Going to the other side, I put her duffle in the back seat before getting into the car myself.

Sweet Vengeance

I drive out and follow the gravel leading out to the main road. Selen sings along to the song on the radio, shocking me with her beautiful singing voice. I glance over at her; she's gazing out the window as the landscape blurs by. Returning my eyes to the road, I'm mesmerized by her voice, almost as if being lured in by a siren.

I pull onto her driveway, a dirt path cut into the woods that hides her house from onlookers. The brown log cabin comes into view as we pull out of the woods. The red shutters are faded from the sun, and the gray paint on the sides is beginning to peel. I come to a stop in front of the porch, and Selen gets out, leading the way into the house after I grab her duffle from the back.

We step inside an average living room: the walls are a light shade of blue, and a black L-shaped couch sits in the center of the room with a coffee table and television across from it, bathed in the sunlight coming through the living room window. To the left side of the room, the whole wall is a bookshelf filled with dozens upon dozens of books. I can see the tiny kitchen sitting near the back of the house. Everything is organized and clean; the blankets are folded and draped over the back of the couch.

Looking back at her as she heads upstairs, she gestures for me to follow as she leads the way to the second floor. My eyes are on her perfect ass the entire way.

Reaching the top step, I notice three solid white doors; she goes to the one straight ahead, which I assume is her bedroom. I follow as she steps into the dark purple room; dark gray hardwood flooring stretches from wall to wall, and in the center of the furthest wall sits a queen bed with a gray comforter set. A gray dresser is pushed against the wall by the door.

"Obviously, this is my room," she says, confirming my theory. Going to the dresser, she pulls out some clothing and gestures for her duffle; I set it on the dresser top for her.

"I figured. Considering you're grabbing clothes out of the dresser drawers. Unless you are stealing someone else's clothing," I sarcastically remark.

"Yeah. Didn't I tell you that I'm a clothing thief?" she replies, chuckling as she places a few items into the duffle. I shake my head with a chuckle before she says, "I... I have something I want to show you. But I'm not sure how you're going to take it."

That can't be good.

"Please don't tell me you have a sacrificial altar or something."

Rolling her eyes and shaking her head, she walks past me out of the bedroom, leading us back into the hallway. She goes to the door on her right side; this one has a passcode deadbolt on it. Whatever was in this room, she did not want anyone unauthorized to see it.

Punching in a quick code, she opens it and steps inside. Following close behind, I find myself walking through darkness; all I can see are shadows of what looks like clutter all around. Bright light blinds me momentarily as she flips a switch. My eyes soon adjust to the sudden change; the cluttered shadows turn into paintings sitting against the walls. A bench table sits alone in the center of the room.

Curious, I walk over to one of the paintings: a sunset on the beach. The artist precisely captured the colors and textures of the waves crashing ashore. In

Sweet Vengeance

the corner of the painting, I notice the SSS signature. Glancing at the paintings, I see the signatures are the same.

"Wow, you're a huge fan," I comment as I walk around the room, admiring each painting until one catches my eye. I stop to study it and find my blue eyes staring back at me as if looking in a mirror. My hand is outstretched, tossing a blade.

Hold on.

"Not quite."

I glance back at her momentarily as she sits on a stool at the table before I check the next painting: it's me drinking a coffee at the local coffee shop. The pieces click into place.

I turn to face her, shock flooding my senses.

"*You* are the artist?" I ask, though I know the answer.

She nods her head and nervously bites her lower lip, which only makes me want to press my lips against hers again.

"Wow. I can't believe it. You're amazing," I add breathlessly, walking the short distance to her.

"This," she says, gesturing around the room, "is my job." She smiles, looking around at all her artwork. "And I love it."

I wrap my arms around her, looking down at her and say, "Your secret is safe with me," before leaning down and pressing my lips to hers, the beautiful, talented artist sitting before me. I always thought I would recognize the artist at first glance if I ever crossed paths with them. I was wrong.

A loud bang echoes through the house as the front door is slammed shut, causing us both to jump away. I immediately reach for my blades, turning toward the bedroom door, when I hear the thud of footsteps pounding up the stairs. I feel Selen's hand gently pushing mine down toward the floor.

"It's okay," she says as I glance back at her. "It's just Jay."

As she says it, the man comes into view. He has jet-black hair pulled back into a ponytail, is about the same height as me, and his ice-blue eyes seem to cut right through me as he comes to a halt at the door. His eyes swing to Selen, glaring at her.

"Do you ever listen to a word I say to you?" he asks harshly, his voice dripping with anger. I glance at Selen to see her cringe beneath his intense glare and harsh words.

Who the hell does he think he is to talk to her like this?

"Uh, why don't we finish this conversation downstairs?" she tells Jay before meeting my eyes. "Rik, you are more than welcome to look around at the paintings some more. I will be right back."

She steps around and past me, her hand softly brushing mine as she moves away, following Jay downstairs. I watch as they vanish from view. I want to take a moment to look at more of the paintings, but suddenly, loud bantering comes from downstairs—they're arguing. Curious, I creep down the steps, my back against the wall that separates the living room from the stairs, hiding me from view as I eavesdrop.

Sweet Vengeance

"You don't realize just how amazing he is," Selen starts, her voice full of emotion. "He is kind, caring, and understanding." I smile, knowing she is talking about me.

"You can't trust him. I am only trying to protect you from getting hurt," Jay says. I can't fault the guy for trying to shield her from getting hurt, but he doesn't even know me.

"And how would you know? You told me that you left him before he was one. How do you know he isn't a great guy? Jay, he has your heart," she says, practically begging him to understand.

Left me? What is she talking about?

"Do you really think I don't remember leaving my *own* son?" I hear the stranger say.

Son? No fucking way.

I bolt down the rest of the steps, shocking Selen and Jay as they turn to face me. Selen's expression turns guilty, and Jay looks like a thief caught robbing a store. Glaring at both of them, my anger rises as I shake uncontrollably.

"SON?" I shout into the awkward silence, staring daggers at this stranger—my supposed father. "So you're the piece of shit that left my mom with a kid to raise on her own?"

Selen takes a step toward me. "It's okay, Rik, just calm down," she says softly. My eyes swing to her with betrayal and hurt.

"Don't you dare come near me," I say harshly. "You knew this entire time?" I practically shout at her, making her wince at my raised voice. She guilty nods her head in answer.

"It wasn't my place to tell you, Rik. I wanted to," she says, her voice breaking. Jay glares at her angrily.

"You weren't even supposed to get close to him. Now look what you did," he sternly tells Selen, who looks like she just got slapped. "And I didn't abandon your mother—"

"You both can go to hell!" I yell as I turn and walk out the front door. I hear the slam behind me, then open again, followed by Selen's footsteps as she runs after me.

"Rik, will you at least let me explain?" she begs, shouting behind me as I walk to my car. I feel her grab my hand and turn around swinging; she ducks under my arm and immediately backs away, letting go.

"Leave me alone," I demand harshly as I open the car door, get in, and rev the engine to life before peeling out of her driveway.

Glancing in the rearview, I see Selen staring after my car, her arms wrapped around her as if hugging herself. It's the last thing I see before the woods engulf me.

I can't believe that she knew. Why would she hide something like that from me? I had the fucking right to know.

The betrayal slams into me hard as I speed down the dirt road.

CHAPTER 25

I don't know how long I stand in the driveway. My heart shatters into a million pieces as I watch his car fade out of view, leaving me hugging myself as the dust settles around me, tears slowly slipping down my cheeks.

What have I done?

When I can no longer feel sorry for myself, I finally return to the house to find Jay sitting on the steps, head in his hands. He looks up at me, his expression a mixture of sorrow and anger.

"Why the hell was he even here?" he demands coldly, his icy blue eyes glued to me in anger, even as I wipe my eyes to regain my composure.

"Because," I begin, snapping, "believe it or not, I actually like him. Maybe even love him," I tell him, my heart beating loudly and painfully in my chest. I never thought it would hurt this much; it was almost unbearable, like I was drowning and unable to come up for oxygen; like the world was crashing in around me.

"What if he was only using you?" Jay asks, studying me.

"Why would you even think that? What has he ever done to you?" I ask angrily, my body heating up as my temper sparks in the center of my chest, the fiery burn of it sizzling just below the surface, aching to be released. "Tell me, Jay, what is your problem with him? He is your flesh and blood, yet here you are talking about him as if he were the enemy."

"I will not explain myself to a selfish, insecure little girl who can't get over her past," he growls. His words pierce me like a dagger to the heart and leave me gaping at him as he stands and walks out the door.

I stare at the empty space as he vanishes, leaving me in disbelief.

Why the hell was all of this falling back onto me? I wasn't the one who disappeared on Rik when he was only a baby; I wasn't the one who told him, and it wasn't my place to tell Rik that I knew Jay was his father. It wasn't like he would believe me, even if I did say something.

My pulse quickens as the anger consumes me inch by inch. The tears of sadness stop as the fiery anger takes over, spreading blazing heat through my veins like a wildfire that cannot be contained. I am panting as the world spins around me. I stagger toward the kitchen; every step seems like an effort as I sway like a drunk. Glancing at the mirror hanging on the wall that hides the staircase from view in the living room, I find a pitiful version of myself staring back, my eyes red-ringed and puffy from crying, stray tears staining my cheeks.

Sweet Vengeance

The colors of the living room vanish into a red haze, almost like fog taking over my vision. Unable to hold it in anymore, I watch in slow motion as my fist collides with the mirror, shattering my reflection to pieces. The broken mirror falls to the floor, the crash echoing through the living room. Turning to the couch, I go full She-Hulk as I send it flying into the bookshelf, causing most of the books to tumble to the floor with loud thuds. I spin, slamming my fist into the sheetrock, leaving a gaping hole, before storming upstairs.

Walking into the bathroom, I grab the scissors out of the top drawer and take chunks of my hair into my fist; the scissors swish, and huge strands fall soundlessly to the floor with every cut. I stare at myself in the mirror with my now chin-length hair, hating the person staring back at me. I stab the scissors into the glass, shattering yet another mirror in my fiery anger, embedding the scissors into the sheetrock wall and pulling out my cell phone. It's time to finish this.

> MEET ME AT THE PARK

I press the send button as I walk down the steps. My phone vibrates a few short moments later when Abe responds.

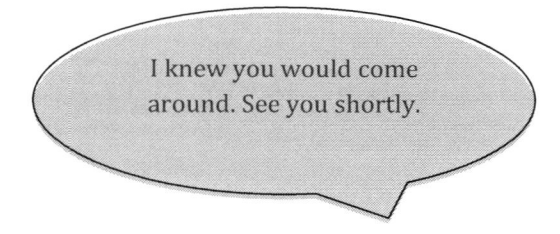

> I knew you would come around. See you shortly.

I read his so-sure-of-himself text before I toss the phone uncaring behind me as I walk outside into the twilight as the sun sets behind the trees. I set off, lost in thoughts.

I'm done caring. I have nothing to live for anymore. I lost the only guy I may have come to love over the last few days, the only guy I was comfortable with, and I even lost the guy who saved me, whom I considered a father. The anger has dissipated, leaving me numb as I walk into the park.

I find Abe leaning against a tree separating the two baseball fields, dressed in a pair of blue jean shorts and a gray polo shirt. His shaggy blonde hair is long enough to fall into his eyes. He smiles when he notices me walking across the grass to him. I stop a few feet away; his eyes travel the length of my body, taking me in.

"You cut your hair. I almost didn't recognize you," he comments, studying my fresh haircut. "You still look gorgeous, of course. But why the sudden text, darling?"

"This ends tonight," I tell him. His gut-wrenching laugh surprises me as he shakes his head in amusement.

"What ends tonight?"

"Your life."

"And you think you can take me?" he asks, still chuckling. "That's a joke, right?"

"You'd be surprised at what I'm capable of now," I snarl at him. "I have changed since the night you raped me."

Sweet Vengeance

His eyes go dark at the mention of that night.

I swing my fist. It cracks across his face, and his head snaps to the side, the blow sending him stumbling back. He looks at me in stunned silence and smiles as he wipes his hand across his bottom lip, dripping with blood.

"You're going to regret that, bitch," he growls as he strides toward me.

I brace myself for his attack as he lowers himself, trying to tackle me. I sidestep, spinning, and plant my foot into his exposed back, knocking him to the ground. Not wasting any time, I wrap my forearm around his neck and brace my other arm as I pull him into a chokehold. He gasps, struggling to pry my arm away from his throat.

Yeah, I got you this time.

But he isn't ready to give up. Abe slams his weight backward, harshly knocking the breath out of me as I hit the ground with him on top of me. I stare at the dark, starless night sky, coughing and gasping to regain my breathing, tears springing to the corner of my eyes.

I push him off as I quickly stumble to stand, my back and ribs throbbing from the impact, sharp pain shooting through me with each breath. I try to brace myself through the ache as he stands up to face me, his eyes boring into mine.

"I really don't understand why you keep fighting it," he says between breaths. "You know that you're attracted to me. And one of these days, you'll realize it and come crawling back, begging me to satisfy your needs."

I stare at him in disbelief and utter surprise that he thinks I would ever forgive him—least of all, have sex with him.

Violet S.R. Cox

"That's never going to happen. You raped me!"

I take a deep breath in before I run at him; my whole body protests in agony at the movement. I throw another punch—it lands. Growling, Abe snaps his attention to me as he approaches, causing me to back-peddle until my back hits the chain link fence. When the soft clinking meets my ears, I realize I'm pinned with no way out. Fear slams into me like a wrecking ball as I watch him close the space that separates us, anger written all over his face as his hand encloses my throat, pushing me against the fence and lifting my feet off the ground. My palms start sweating as panic and dread overtake me.

This is how I die.

CHAPTER 26
Alarik's POV

My father has been right under my nose this whole entire time, and I never even knew it. I only know what my mom told me when I asked about my father: that he left when I was still a baby, saying something about wanting me to have a normal childhood.

So why didn't he return home when Mom was diagnosed with stage-four colon cancer? He should have been there helping me take care of her. But no, it was *me* who held her hand and supported her. The chemotherapy was brutal. She started off feeling great the first few months, until one day, she couldn't even get out of bed; from there, she grew weaker with every day that passed. She started puking up everything she ate, unable to keep anything down, shedding weight until she was nothing but skin and bones.

The stern and loving woman I once knew was withering away right before my eyes, and all I could do was give her the morphine she was prescribed. But that barely touched her pain, and she would still cry. I wanted so badly to take her pain away, and I felt useless because there was nothing more I could do.

Violet S.R. Cox

The last few days were the hardest to endure as I watched my once-strong mother lose control of her arms, unable to hold her spoon and fumbling, trying to feed herself, wearing most of her food. I was the one who spoon-fed her until she passed away. I was the one who held her hand when she took her last breath. I was the one who had to call hospice to inform them that she passed away. I was the one who had to wait for them to arrive, and I was the one who had to watch them wheel her out in a black body bag.

All the while, my father hid away by his own choice.

I was only a teenager; it wasn't my job, but it became my responsibility since my father was hiding. I don't regret a single moment of taking care of her, but I really could have used the help.

Angrily, I wipe the tears away.

Calming down, I turn the car around and head back toward Selen's, knowing my mom would be disappointed with how I treated her. Selen didn't tell me because it wasn't her place to, and I probably wouldn't have believed her if she tried. I can't believe I wanted to hit her; at least she was fast enough to dodge, but it doesn't matter. I should have never raised my hand to her; my mom raised me better than that.

My mother, *not my father.*

The look of hurt in Selen's eyes as she stood reflected in the rearview mirror, staring after my car, haunted me.

Damn it, I royally fucked up.

Sweet Vengeance

I pull into Selen's driveway, stopping in front of the porch to find the front door wide open. I leave the car, walk to the front door, and abruptly stop as I peer through the entryway. Panic floods my body as I look at the destroyed living room. The couch is upside down and against the now broken bookshelf.

What the hell happened? Where is Selen? Is she okay?

I pull out a blade as I walk into the house; stepping into the living room, I notice the hole in the wall and the shattered mirror, with crimson drops of blood leading to the stairs. I follow the trail up to the bathroom. I'm surprised to find a pair of scissors embedded in the sheetrock where the mirror once sat, now in broken pieces on the small vanity. Long dark strands of her hair lay scattered beneath it.

I pick up a strand from the sink, rubbing her hair between my fingers as fear of the worse floods my mind. *I have to find her.*

Dropping the piece of hair, I turn on my heels and check the other two rooms; she isn't in either.

Pulling out my cell phone, I dial her number and quickly descend the stairs. The awful ringtone breaks the silence. Spinning toward the direction of the sound, I realize it is coming from near the couch; I rush over, worried she may be under it. My eyes land on the purple of her phone case, which is just beside the couch. I scoop it up in my hand as I hang up.

I swipe her phone open—thank God she doesn't have a security pin—to find a text she sent moments after I left.

It was sent to Abe.

No, no, no! She was going after him alone, and it was my fault; the realization slams into my gut like a heavy punch.

I have to save her.

I rush out the door and to my car. Slamming it in gear, I spin the car around and speed toward the park. *Please don't be too late.* The trees rip by as tires squeal with every sudden sharp turn.

I pull up to see two dark figures on the baseball field. One is suspended in the air as if they are hovering. I recognize it as Selen being held by her throat. I slam the car in park as I bolt out of the car and dash toward her, slamming my shoulder into Abe's side and tackling him to the ground, causing him to release his grip. I hear her coughing harshly as she gulps in the fresh oxygen.

Immediately, I stand, kicking Abe in the head and knocking him out before returning my attention to Selen, who is on all fours, breathing hard and rubbing her throat. Her hair now ends at her chin.

So she did cut it. But why?

"What the fuck were you thinking?" I demand, walking toward her.

Her glare meets mine as she looks up from the ground, the moon revealing her usually bright eyes, now darker, reflecting sorrow in their depths. Instead of answering me, she stands up, turns, and walks away.

"Selen, answer me," I snap, following her and grabbing her shoulder.

The sudden force surprises me as Selen sends me flying away from her. I hit the ground hard, knocking the breath out of me, and stare up at her.

Sweet Vengeance

Ouch… So, don't touch her while she's like this. Got it.

"Why the fuck do you even care?" she coldly asks. "You're the one who left, not me!" She's fighting back tears; I can hear it in the way her voice breaks.

She turns to walk away as I search for the right words. "Because I screwed up," I call after her, quickly standing up from the ground. She stops her back still to me, waiting for what I have to say as if to consider it's worth sticking around.

At least she stopped, so don't screw this up. Be careful what you say.

"I came back to your house to apologize for how I acted and treated you. But instead, I found your house destroyed and my girlfriend missing." I hear her catch her breath before slowly turning to face me. "I should have never swung at you. It won't ever happen again."

"What did you just say?" she asks, almost as if confused or dazed, though her gaze is intense as it meets mine.

"That I should have never swung on you?"

"No, before that. What did—what did you call me?" she stumbles over her words a little, but her eyes don't waver.

"Girlfriend," I say as I take a slow step toward her, unsure if she'll send me on my ass again. "I realized after leaving that I love you and don't want to lose you." I see the look of surprise in her eyes, and she goes speechless. She glances at the ground, looking away from me; I don't sense violence in her anymore.

I close the remaining distance and carefully grab her face in my hand, turning and tilting her face to look up at me. "I'm sorry, Selen. I didn't mean to hurt you," I whisper as I wipe away her tears as they spring up. I press a kiss against her forehead, pulling her into a hug. She reluctantly buries her face into my shoulder.

"You love me?" she asks in a whisper.

"Yes."

She goes silent for a moment as I glance back to ensure Abe hasn't woken up yet. "We should get out of here before he wakes up," I tell her, leading her toward the still-running car. I open the door for her, and she slides into the passenger seat. Once in the driver seat, I put the car in gear and leave the park.

"What you did wa—"

"Don't. Even. Say. It!" she growls slowly through clenched teeth, glaring at me, making me fall silent and cringe inwardly. "I know what I did was stupid, but at that given moment, I didn't give a shit if I lived or died. Between you and Jay going off on me, I wasn't in my right mind. Leave it at that."

"What do you mean he went off on you? What for?" I ask. When the streetlights and headlights bounce off of her, I can see the exhaustion in her eyes; they're heavy, and as her eyes start closing, she leans her head against the window.

"Because I let you into my life," she mumbles as she drifts to sleep.

I look over at her sleeping form, angry at Jay—not just for leaving me but for Selen's sake. She didn't deserve either one of us snapping at her.

Sweet Vengeance

Pulling into her driveway, I stop in front of the porch. The front door is still open, and the interior light shines through the crack.

I scoop up the sleeping Selen out of the car, carrying her petite, slender body into the house, where I find Jay standing in the middle of the wrecked living room. He turns when he hears my footsteps. When his eyes land on Selen in my arms, they go wide with worry.

"Is she okay?" he asks, walking over to us. He comes to a stop just before me, his eyes scanning Selen's body for any wounds before he turns his attention to me. "What happened?"

"She'll be fine," I say. "But thanks to both of us, she nearly got herself killed tonight." I start up the steps, trying to keep my temper at bay so I don't wake her.

Jay follows me upstairs, more out of concern for her than nervousness about what I could possibly do. I notice him stop in front of the bathroom door, where he sees the shattered mirror and strands of hair on the vanity.

Leaving him there, I walk into Selen's bedroom. I lay her down gently on the mattress and pull the covers over her body. Quietly leaving the room, I silently shut the door behind me and meet Jay's eyes before walking down the stairs. Walking through the hazardous living room, I enter the kitchen and search for a few trash bags.

"What are you searching for?" he asks as he watches.

"Trash bags. I won't leave my girlfriend to clean up all the mess we caused," I snap, glaring at him. He looks taken back for a split second as he goes silent and glances around the living room.

"Under the sink. Girlfriend? Since when?" he asks, studying me like a protective father. Funny how he acts this way when she isn't his blood, yet he didn't want to meet me, his own child; the anger begins slipping through.

"Honestly, why the fuck does it matter?" I coldly ask. "You're angry with her, and you hate your son." He doesn't seem affected by the ice in my voice or glare.

"It's not like that, Rik," he starts, sighing.

"I don't care," I tell him as I grab a few trash bags and walk into the living room to begin picking up shards of glass from the shattered mirror.

"I understand. When you want an explanation, I am here," he says as he walks over to the couch and moves it back to its original location.

We pick up the living room in silence, and I keep glancing over at him, comparing his looks to mine. I know without a doubt that he is my father, with his jet-black hair and blue eyes matching mine.

Chapter 27

I wake up in the comfort of my bed, unsure of how I got there, sitting up and looking around my emptied room. The last thing I remember is Rik saving my life, telling me he loved me, and calling me his girlfriend. He was driving me home when I must have fallen asleep. How long have I been asleep, and where is he?

Dragging myself out of bed, I, unfortunately, have a mess to clean up from my rampage. Walking to the bathroom, I find it clean; the missing mirror is the only sign of anything being out of the ordinary. Even the hair I chopped off is gone.

Weird. Guess I'll work on the living room then. I head down the steps and hear the hushed voices of two men talking; I stop and eavesdrop.

"Look, I love Selen, and you need to accept that. What would be so wrong in getting to know your son?" I recognize the voice as Rik's; the person he is talking to has to be Jay.

So they couldn't get along earlier and even blamed me.

"Okay, maybe we can get to know each other," Jay says.

Taking a deep breath, I walk the rest of the way down the steps, walking into the living room to find both of them sitting on the couch, which is back in its original spot.

Two sets of blue eyes land on me as I enter; ignoring them, I glance around the already-cleaned living room. The only signs of disturbance are the broken bookshelves and the hole where I put my fist through the wall earlier.

Feeling the weight of their eyes on me, I turn to find Jay taking in my short hair. I walk past them and into the kitchen, not wanting to talk to either one. I hear them stand up as I open the fridge, pulling out a bottle of water.

"Selen, sweetie, are you okay?" Jay asks. I turn, glaring at him, still hurt and angry by what he said earlier.

"Why the hell do you care? The last thing you said to me was that you wouldn't explain yourself to a selfish and insecure little girl," I hiss at him, doing air quotes with my fingers. "So, please explain why you care about my well-being now?"

Jay looks taken back, with guilt glistening in his eyes—Rik steps around the couch.

"Selen, babe. Why don't you just give—"

"No!" I cut Rik off. "You don't have that right. Neither one of you has the *fucking* right to try and make me feel guilty. Not after what both of *you* said to me. Not after *you* put all the blame back on me. I didn't do anything to deserve how you both treated me."

Sweet Vengeance

Both Rik and Jay stand there in shock at my outburst.

"We know," they say in unison as they stare at me, worried.

Alarik walks into the kitchen and stops in front of me. He puts a folded finger under my chin, lifting my face to look into those breathtaking blue eyes. I see the guilt, sadness, and love in them, almost making me feel guilty for snapping.

"How are you feeling?" he asks, his eyes searching mine for the truth.

"Fine. But a little confused about how my house got cleaned," I reply as I look around the house. "I could have sworn I destroyed it in a rage."

"Rage?" he asks, confused.

"Yeah. For immortals, when our emotions—especially anger—get the best of us, we lose control and go into a powerful rage," Jay explains calmly, his eyes meeting mine, then Rik's, who half turns to look at him.

"Oh, well, that explains the bomb that went off here," Rik comments before he turns to me. "I figured that cleaning it up was the least I could do since I was part of the reason for it getting destroyed in the first place." He pulls me into a hug and adds, "Jay helped, too. We feel guilty for taking our anger out on you."

"None of it was your fault," Jay says. "It wasn't your place to tell him, and it wasn't fair of me to try to restrict you from him. But I am glad you're stubborn and found someone you can trust. You deserve it. Both of you do." He smiles at the sight of me in Rik's arms. "I just hope you both can forgive me one day."

I pull out of Rik's encircled arms. "Look, Jay, you're the closest thing I have to father. Of course I forgive you," I say, "but don't ever let it happen again." Surprise passes through his face as he meets my eyes with a soft smile before nodding in agreement.

"I'm going to head home and let you two talk. Let me know if you need anything," Jay says as he turns and heads toward the front door. But he stops at the threshold and says, "Selen, I like your hair like that."

"Uh, thanks," I say, running my hand self-consciously through my short hair.

The door opens and closes behind him, leaving just Rik and I, who pulls me against him.

"You look hot with short hair," he comments as his hand strokes a strand of my hair, his knuckles brushing against my cheek, sending a warm shiver through me.

"I didn't with long hair?" I ask playfully, arching an eyebrow; a look of *Oh shit, I just put my foot in my own mouth* passes over his face, making me laugh.

"No, that's not what I meant," he says, staring into my eyes. "You're beautiful either way. But that could just be because I love you."

I catch my breath at his words; he pulls me close against him and leans down, pressing his lips to mine. It's not a hungry or heated kiss—this one is more gentle, just the simple brush of lips against one another, almost like an apology.

"I don't really know what love feels like, but if this is it, then I think I love you too," I whisper, pulling away and looking up at him. "But are you sure you want me as your girlfriend?" I don't understand why he would, but he pulls back with a look that says *are you crazy?*

"Yes, I'm sure. Why wouldn't I?" he replies, smiling down at me. "You're amazing, beautiful, and talented. Oh, and let's not forget that you can cook."

"Oh, so you like me cause of my cooking?" I question, arching my eyebrow in amusement.

"Love, and it doesn't hurt," he corrects me, smiling as he places a kiss on my forehead.

I grin before walking into the living room with Rik following me, and we sit down. He pulls me close as I put on a movie. I curl up beside him, his arm over my shoulder and my head resting against his.

About halfway through the movie, I can feel the exhaustion overtake me as I drift to sleep in the safety of his warm arms.

I momentarily wake as he lays me on my bed and feel the covers draping over me. I look at the edge of the bed to see his figure turn to leave.

"Rik. Please don't leave. Stay with me, please?" I ask him sleepily. He turns to look at me in the darkness; the moonlight shining through the window shows the surprise on his face.

"Are you sure?" he asks cautiously.

"Yes. Come on," I say, gesturing to the spot beside me on the bed.

Violet S.R. Cox

Rik carefully walks to that side, stripping out of his jeans and t-shirt, before crawling under the covers with me. Laying on his back, he scoots closer and brings me close, which I gratefully accept. My head is on his warm chest, rising and falling gently under me as I listen to the steady beat of his heart. My arm drapes over him, and I slide one leg between his as I fit my body against him.

Wrapped in his warmth, his fingers stroke my hair, slowly lulling me back to sleep.

Chapter 28
Alarik's POV

The following day, when I open my eyes, I find her still asleep, curled up on her side facing me; her chest softly rises and falls as she slumbers, looking peaceful. I feel a smile form as I stare at her beauty.

To think that I almost lost her last night... I have never felt pure terror like I did when I walked back into the wrecked living room. I never knew I could care this much about someone, not since roping my heart off, but Selen somehow broke the barrier from around me.

And now I was hopelessly in love with her.

I slowly get out of bed, careful not to wake her, knowing she needs rest. I grab my jeans and t-shirt off the floor before I creep out of the bedroom, feeling like a teenager sneaking around having sex as I walk into the bathroom to get dressed.

Violet S.R. Cox

I head down the stairs, thinking this might be a good time for Jay and I to talk. I remember what Selen told me about her ability to read minds and communicate mentally if she thought of them. I take a deep breath, deciding to try it, concentrating on nothing but him.

"Jay, can we talk?" I envision pushing the question out, kind of like outgoing mail.

"Yeah, I'll be over shortly." I hear his voice in my head, causing me to jump a little at the sudden reply. I had doubts about it working, but they were clearly wrong.

"Selen is still asleep; just let yourself in. I'll be in the kitchen," I mentally send back as I walk into the kitchen. Opening the fridge to find mostly water and a few bottles of Gatorade, I grab one and take a long swig of the sweet, refreshing liquid that runs over my tongue and quenches my thirst. I seal it and set it on the round gray kitchen table.

I search the kitchen for pancake mix and eggs. Pulling the supplies out, the door near the kitchen opens and closes quietly. Glancing back, I see Jay walk into the kitchen dressed in gray sweats and a black t-shirt, and his hair, which we happen to share, is pulled back in a bun. His icy-blue eyes study me carefully as if trying to understand my thoughts or feelings.

"Hey, what's up?" he asks as I crack a few eggs into a pan.

"I was wondering if we could talk about everything. To be honest, I have a lot of questions," I tell him as I scramble the eggs together.

Sweet Vengeance

"That's understandable," he tells me as he pours some pancake mix into a mixing bowl, adds water, and then stirs it. "What question do you want to start with?" he asks as he hands me the bowl of pancake batter.

"Were you immortal before or after I was born?" I drop a few spoonfuls of batter onto the griddle.

"Yes. I was turned years before I met your mom," he answers. Opening the fridge, he grabs a bottle of water. I flip the pancakes and finish cooking the scrambled eggs.

"How did you die?" I ask him as I grab two plates, putting pancakes and eggs on both. I hand him a plate and gesture toward the kitchen table.

Jay pulls two forks out of the drawer next to the sink and the syrup out of the cabinet above the stove before coming to the table. He sits across from me, pouring syrup on his pancakes, then hands me the bottle.

"It was June 6, 1944."

I look up at him in surprise.

"D-Day?" I ask. He nods with a solemn look as he remembers that day. I can tell that it still haunts him.

"I was one of thousands of soldiers that landed on Omaha Beach. The Germans were hiding atop the cliffs that overlooked that beach, prepared for us. Before we even started storming the beach, we were greeted by gunfire. Once we landed, fellow soldiers fell left and right around me. It was a bloody slaughter. The beach and water ran red with blood." Jay starts to look distant as he gets lost in the memory. "I was trying to help one of my brothers-in-arms who was injured when I got shot. I was bleeding out onto the already blood-drenched sand."

"Who saved you?" I ask, still in shock.

"That I don't know. All I really remember from that day is all the blood, the sound of gunfire, the screams of agony around me, getting shot, and bleeding out. And then waking up confused surrounded by several of my brother's dead bodies. It took me several years to even discover that I was immortal," he explains, with sorrow in his eyes.

"How did you meet mom?" I ask curiously, trying to change the subject to stop that horrific day going through his mind.

"I met your mother on November 17, 1992," he starts, a smile forming on his face. "She was breathtakingly beautiful with her long blonde hair and those hazel eyes that seemed to see right through me. I met her at a bar that I used to frequent. I fell in love with her instantly. She wasn't just beautiful; she had brains and amazed me with everything she talked about. We dated for a few months, then I proposed to her."

"Did she know you were an immortal?"

"Yes, she knew something was different about me and immediately figured it out," he says, his eyes lighting up as he speaks fondly of her. "When we found out she was pregnant with you, we were overjoyed. I still remember the day you were born; your mom was in labor for twenty-eight hours. You came into the world on September 15, 1994, at three in the morning, weighing seven pounds and eleven ounces. You were beautiful and healthy; there was nothing more we could ask for." As he tells the story, I can see the love he holds deep inside him.

Sweet Vengeance

"But my fear of potentially ruining your life loomed over my head, so I thought it was best to leave. I wanted you to live a normal life before I dragged you into the immortal part of it. I didn't want anyone to target you. I thought I was doing the right thing. I am so sorry, Rik."

I see the glimmer of tears he is trying to fight back as he locks eyes with me.

"I can understand your reasoning," I reply. "But I was only seventeen when Mom got diagnosed with cancer. I was the one who took care of her. I had to watch her wither away before my eyes, and I couldn't do anything to help her." Tears begin to well up in my own eyes. "When she passed away, I was all alone with no one to talk to."

"I know, and I will never forgive myself for that. That is one of my biggest regrets. I should have been there to help; you shouldn't have done it all alone. I am so sorry, son," Jay says as a tear slides down his cheek. "What did she tell you about me?"

"That you left to protect us, that you were in trouble and didn't want it showing up on our doorstep," I tell him. "I understand why you left. It doesn't mean that I have to like it, though."

"Why aren't you mad at me anymore?" he asks in confusion as he studies me.

"Because I already lost one parent, and I just found my other parent. I'd rather try to get to know my father instead of living in anger and missing out on time," I explain, shrugging. "Is there anything else I should know?"

"There's one more thing that may help you understand yourself."

"Which would be?" I ask nervously.

"You are part immortal, which is why you can block your thoughts without trying, why you heal quicker compared to others, and why you catch onto the thoughts of others," he explains. I feel shocked as he names off all the things I could never figure out all this time.

"I'm half-immortal?" I ask in shock, trying to comprehend this new life-changing information.

"Yes."

I sit there silent for a few moments as I process my whole life. I always healed faster than others but didn't think much of it. As far as reading other people's thoughts, I thought I had this sixth sense. This explained a lot.

"Did you leave Mom money?" I ask, trying to pull myself out of the shock.

"Yes, I always sent her money to help her care for you," Jay explains.

I remember checking the mail a few times to find an envelope addressed to Mom, with the name Jason Samuels on the return address section. It's all slowly starting to make sense.

"You are Jason Samuels," I say, causing him to nod in response. "Who left me the inheritance money?"

"Your mom invested in a life insurance policy to make sure you were set. I was the one who opened the account for you," he explains.

Sweet Vengeance

    My father was in my life, just at a distance. He never truly abandoned me, as I thought. Everything he has done was to protect me and give me the childhood he felt I deserved. As the missing pieces click into place, creating the whole picture, I realize that all of it makes sense.

Chapter 29

 I'm on a beach covered with blood, so much blood. Loud gunshots, explosions, and screams of agony surround me as I run with others dressed in olive green uniforms and matching metal helmets. The smell of sulfur and the stench of blood floods my nostrils, causing my stomach to twist in knots.

 Soldiers all around me fall as bullets tear into their bodies. The shots are coming from the cliffs surrounding the beachfront, overlooking it. Bodies lay in pools of their own blood, scattered unmoving all over the wet sandy beach as more soldiers pass them, running toward the cliffs. Glancing down at my hands, I find myself holding a rifle with the ammunition clip-fed through the top. I have never seen a gun like this.

 I jolt awake, panting and drenched in sweat as my heart races. *What the hell was that?* I had never seen that place; it was like something out of a war movie. The distinctive stench of blood and sulfur, the sight of bodies brutally shot down, and the loud sound of gunfire have all followed me from the dream, haunting me in the world of the living. This nightmare felt so real, almost as if I was reliving it.

Catching my breath and steadying my racing heart, I glance over where Rik fell asleep last night to find the side of the bed empty. He must have woken up early and let me sleep in.

Sighing and trying to shake the nightmare away, I leave bed and head downstairs, still baffled. I walk into the living room and find Rik and Jay talking at the kitchen table. They both glance up at my presence.

"Morning, babe," Rik greets me as I walk to the kitchen. He gets up, grabs a drink from the fridge, puts something on a plate, and sets it on the table, gesturing for me to sit. "Eat."

Confused, I do as instructed, looking at the plate to find pancakes and scrambled eggs, making my stomach grumble.

"Morning," I grumble in response, still not fully awake.

"Give her a little bit. She takes a while to wake up," Jay explains to Rik as his eyes scan my body, ensuring I am visibly okay, which he has done since the night he saved me.

I take a bite of the scrambled eggs and am welcomed by a cheesy explosion.

"So, how did you sleep?" Rik asks.

Violet S.R. Cox

"I was sleeping really good until I had a strange nightmare. This one was new, and I'd never seen the place before," I mumble, shrugging as I take another bite of my breakfast.

"What was it about?" Jay asks, his eyes weighing on me.

"I'm not exactly sure. All I know is I was on a beach covered in blood. I heard the sound of gunfire and saw what looked like soldiers falling all around me as they got shot. I was also holding a rifle," I explain.

Looking up, I find both of them staring at me in surprise. Jay glances away from me as if he's guilty of something, and Rik flashes him a look.

"What?" I ask with a nervous chuckle as confusion floods me, the fork hanging in mid-air before I set it back down.

"I'm so sorry, Selen," Jay says.

"For what?"

"I must have somehow pulled you into one of my memories. I didn't mean to, sweetie," Jay explains, his eyes full of sorrow. I find myself shocked as I stare at him.

"Hold up. Your memories?" I ask as I process what I saw, stunned to learn something new about my mentor, who was always quiet about his past. "You were a soldier? And you went through all that?"

Jay solemnly nods; I glance over Rik, still in a daze.

Sweet Vengeance

"He was one of the soldiers who invaded Omaha Beach on D-Day," Rik says.

I sit there silent momentarily before returning my eyes to Jay's. "How old were you?" I ask before I can stop myself.

"Twenty-five," he answers.

"That was also the day he was turned," Rik continues, surprising me more; I quickly do the math in my head.

"So you're actually ninety-four years old? Well, you look good for an old man," I joke, trying to lighten his mood. Rik bursts out laughing, and Jay chuckles, shaking his head and smiling.

"Yes, Selen. I am technically ninety-four. And old," he replies cheerfully; the joke did the trick.

"Hold up. I've been training with you for the last two years and am just learning this about you. Guess I have been replaced as your favorite," I say, pretending to pout as I cross my arms over my chest.

Chuckling, Jay shakes his head. "You'll always be my favorite daughter I never had," he reassures me.

"More like your only," I say, rolling my eyes as I take the last bite of my food. "So, what else did I miss?" I ask as I glance between the two of them and sip my water.

"Well, I am apparently half-immortal," Rik tells me, making me choke on the water in surprise.

Finally, after some teary coughing and Rik rubbing my back, I regain my breathing.

"You are?" I ask, my voice sounding coarse from the hacking. Rik smiles, nodding his head. "Wow. I guess that would explain why I could never get any of your thoughts."

The three of us sit at the table talking. Jay tells me how he fell in love with Alarik's mom and how she was beautiful and intelligent. Rik tells me about his mother and how she passed from cancer, making my heart ache for him.

I keep glancing between the two, comparing their looks; Rik is definitely Jay's son. There was no denying it. He has the same jet-black hair. His eyes are a shade darker than Jay's, but they both have the same way of holding themselves.

We soon find ourselves laughing and talking about random things. And for the first time, I feel like part of a family. I look at Jay before glancing at Rik.

"What do you think about seeing if your son can keep up with our training?" I ask Jay as I meet Rik's stormy-blue eyes, egging him on.

"Is that a challenge, Miss Selen?" he asks, arching an eyebrow in amusement as he leans forward in his chair.

"Nah, not at all. I don't think you could handle it," I reply as I lean back in the chair.

"You don't think so?" Rik asks, chuckling. Next to him, Jay is just shaking his head at both of us, like a father listening to an argument between teenagers. "You're on. I don't want to hear any crying when I beat your ass."

Sweet Vengeance

"Oh really?" I purr, raising an eyebrow at him. "Just remember this pretty little sweet thing has some spice to her."

"This should be interesting," Jay comments as he eyes us both, trying to figure out if he should intervene or let it play out.

I quickly change into my training clothes, put on my shoes, and head toward the training field.

Chapter 30

Arriving at the training field, I turn and look at Alarik, who is stunned entirely silent at the sight of our training field. His eyes scan the entire area, examining every obstacle. I give him a few moments to take it all in and turn to Jay.

"I was thinking, for Rik and I to be able to take Abe out as a team, that it would probably be best for us to fight against you. That way, we can learn to work together," I explain. Jay leans against a tree, thinking it through.

"That's not a bad idea," he replies. "But I won't be taking it easy on you."

"I don't want you to," I reply. "We aren't going to learn if you do."

Finished with admiring the course, Rik walks over to us to join in the conversation.

Sweet Vengeance

"So, what is the plan?" Rik asks, looking between Jay and me.

"Um, how about you and I do the obstacle course while Jay comes up with a plan for our training with him?" I suggest. Jay nods in agreement, and Rik smiles as if this will be a simple task. "It isn't as easy as it looks," I warn Rik, who shrugs.

"Are we racing to see who can make it to the end first?" he asks, almost excitedly.

"Now, this I have to see," Jay comments with an amused head shake.

"Well, you can tell us when to start then," I say, looking at Jay. "That way, there's no cheating."

Rik and I make our way to the start of the course. "Are you sure you can handle this?" I ask him as I stretch; his eyes admire my body in my workout clothes: black yoga pants, a purple crop top, and sneakers.

"I'm looking forward to beating that fine ass of yours," he replies, smiling seductively at me, causing me to roll my eyes at him.

"We'll see about that."

"READY?" Jay shouts.

I back away from the starting line, knowing I'll need a running start. Rik glances back at me, confused.

"SET."

Violet S.R. Cox

I lower myself toward the ground for maximum acceleration.

"GO!"

I launch myself off my back foot and spring forward. Passing Rik in an instant, I plant my foot against the wooden wall, pushing myself up and grabbing the edge. I pull myself up and over, the wood digging into my soft palms. Glancing back, I see Rik's hand gripping the edge before I drop to the other side with a dull thud, landing smoothly. Rik not-so-gracefully lands beside me as he falls on his ass.

I bolt toward the monkey bars. Rik's pounding footsteps ring out behind me as I climb the ladder; he reaches it just as I grab the first bar and swing away. When I make it to the end, I hear Rik's heavy breathing following me. I quickly descend the ladder.

I hear the soft thud as Rik lands next to me. We share a glance, our eyes drawing each other in. Both of us are breathing hard, but since he isn't used to this course, he's breathing even harder.

I smile before I take off running for the last obstacle: the rope climb. I grab the rope, entwining it around my legs, and pull myself up, one hand in front of the other as my arms burn. Rik is on the rope beside me, only a little lower than me.

"Hey, hon, just a little advice. Don't fall," I sarcastically remark between harsh breaths. "It literally hurts like hell."

"Oh, I would have never guessed that in a million years," he pants as he glares up at me.

Sweet Vengeance

We're nearly evenly matched as I reach the top, and he arrives only seconds after me. We look at each other, knowing that whoever makes it down first wins.

We start to descend; we are both neck and neck. Rik stops and looks at me, smiling when we are dangling about ten feet above the ground.

"I win," he says as he lets go of the rope and drops to the ground.

Shaking my head, I slide down the remaining distance, my feet landing softly on the solid ground. I let go of the rope and look down at Rik, lying there gasping for breath from the sudden impact.

"Cheater," I mutter, crossing my arms over my chest. "Serves you right." I smirk down at him, which earns me a glare and the middle finger. I shake my head and hear Jay chuckling as he does the same.

"I still won," Rik says, breathless, sticking his tongue out at me.

"Yeah, but how sore are you?" I ask, laughing as he stands up, groaning like an old man. "Oh, come on. You sound older than Jay!" I tease him playfully, eliciting another glare and more laughter from Jay. "I told you falling hurts."

"Yeah, yeah," Rik mutters, limping behind me as we approach Jay.

"You are both well matched. You keep up with each other pretty well," he starts. "And take falls pretty gracefully." He flashes a playful grin at Rik, who is finally beginning to recover from the sudden impact.

"Here's the plan," Jay says, leading the way to the sparring mats. "You're both going to fight against me. The goal is to bring me down."

Violet S.R. Cox

Rik and I both nod in agreement.

We take our positions on the mats before Jay, who looks at ease. Rik and I run forward at the same time, crashing into each other and falling to the ground. He lands on top of me, the simple contact sending my senses blazing and forcing me to catch my breath. I see the spark in his eyes as he stands, knowing he felt it, too. He offers me his hand and helps me stand up.

"I said take *me* out, not each other," Jay snaps, bringing us back to the training session. "You have to anticipate each other's moves."

Rik and I separate as we ready ourselves again. I sprint forward, and Rik is behind me; I swing my fist. Jay grabs my outstretched arm and pushes me back into Rik, sending us both crashing to the mats again. I move into a sitting position off of Rik, who groans as he gets back to his feet. I study Jay, trying to think of a way to get through his defenses.

"You have to learn each other's weaknesses and strengths and use them to your advantage," Jay instructs patiently, observing us. I stand slowly, scrutinizing his posture.

I slowly circle to his other side, where he separates Rik and me. Jay glances between us, anticipating who will make the first move. I nod at Rik, and he runs toward Jay while I rush him from behind. Rik leaps, going high, and I strike low, kicking my leg in front of me, hoping to trip Jay. But Jay ducks and spins, jumping over my leg. Rik crashes onto the mat behind me; I stand up and swing my fist at Jay, who blocks with his arm, his other fist colliding with my stomach. I stumble back, the breath knocked out of me momentarily as I gasp in the air. I can feel the bruise already forming.

Sweet Vengeance

"Rik, I have an idea. Block Jay out of your mind," I say telepathically, keeping my eyes locked on Jay.

"Shit, don't do that without warning me." His husky voice is in my head as we circle Jay.

"Warning," I add sarcastically through the link. *"You go for his top half, and I'll go for his legs."*

"Got it."

I run toward Jay, sliding to a stop. *"Now,"* I send, wrapping my legs around Jay's and twisting to the side, making him stumble and almost fall. Rik quickly tackles him into the ground beside me.

Releasing him, Rik stands up and extends his hand to me, helping me up.

"Not bad. You used the mind link, didn't you?" Jay asks, looking at me surprised.

"Yeah," I answer.

Jay smiles like a father proud of his child's accomplishments. "Good. You can't keep hiding from it forever, Selen. You eventually have to come to terms with it and embrace it. It might be the only way to succeed."

"Yeah, yeah. I know," I say, and Rik glances between us, confused. "I'm going to call it a day. If you want to continue, have at it." When Rik looks at me with concern, I add, "I'm fine. Just need a little rest."

Violet S.R. Cox

"I think if Jay is okay with it, I'm going to stay and learn a few more things. I'll be back shortly," he says, looking at Jay, who nods in answer. Rik kisses my cheek before I leave the two of them training.

Walking through the woods to the house, I get lost in thought. I know Jay is right. I do need to accept the fact that I am immortal. But I am still in denial. For me to accept being immortal meant I had to admit that I was raped, which I didn't want to do; I couldn't accept the fact that I was a victim.

I had gotten stronger in the last two years, but if I hope to take Abe out, I must come to terms with it. I need the whole me to make this work. But the fear of losing my human self lingers deep within me, waiting to be overcome. If I don't, more innocent women's lives will be destroyed.

Sweet Vengeance

CHAPTER 31
Alarik's POV

I watch Selen's sexy round ass sway back and forth in the skin-tight yoga pants as she heads home. Whatever Jay said to her seemed to dampen her mood, and I could see the mental battle raging in her eyes before she left.

Turning back to Jay, still confused about what they were talking about, I notice his gaze glued to the spot she disappeared through, with a look of pity in his eyes.

"What does Selen need to accept?" I ask, causing his eyes to turn to me.

Taking a deep breath, he sits down cross-legged on the mats.

"She hasn't really accepted that she died the night Abe—" he stops short, perhaps unsure if I knew the truth of what happened to Selen.

"I know. She told me a while ago. Abe raped her," I say through gritted teeth, enraged at the thought of anyone hurting the beautiful Selen.

Back in school, Selen kept to herself, was quiet, and usually drew or read a book. She had never done anything to anyone. I lost count of how many times I found her in the library, pacing through the stacks in search of her next book to read. Even during lunch, she would sit on the ground, leaning back against the dirty brick wall with a book in her hand. Now that I know of her past, it makes sense she was trying to escape the reality of her cruel home life.

"Well, she wasn't just raped. You know that, right?" Jay asks, bringing me back to the present conversation. "She was also abused by him after he raped her."

"She did tell me he left her with internal bleeding."

"That's what killed her," he explains, his eyes going distant as if he is remembering that night. "She started coughing up a lot of blood."

"Can you show me?" I ask him nervously, wanting to know more about what she endured.

"Are you sure? It's pretty bad," Jay warns me, studying my eyes as if to check my intent.

I nod my head.

"Okay."

Jay closes his eyes and concentrates.

Sweet Vengeance

I am in a car, the headlights shining on the dirt road when they land on someone. A slender body lays motionless off toward the side of the road. Coming to a stop, I get out of the car and rush to the body; it's a young girl curled up in the fetal position, her dark brown hair tangled and obscuring her face. She's wrapped in a dirty, torn dress, revealing pale skin covered in black and blue bruises.

I kneel beside her when I see her eyes move, looking up at me.

"Miss, oh my God. What happened?" I ask her, shock filling my voice; well, Jay's voice, technically.

"Who are you?" she asks, sounding broken, hurt, and weak. "Did he send you to kill me?"

I study her, confused as I scan her body, taking in her injuries. I reach out to her, causing her to jerk away in fear. I watch my love grit her teeth from the pain she awakes from the movement. I quickly withdraw my hand, not wanting to make things worse.

"It's okay. It's okay. I am not here to hurt you, miss. I live down the road," I explain to her, pointing down the road. "I saw you out here and stopped. My name is Jay Samuels." I reach into my pocket, pulling out my cell phone. "I'm going to call for help."

"Don't," she says weakly. "There is no point."

"Why not?"

Violet S.R. Cox

"They won't make it in time," she starts to explain as she gags, coughing up an alarming amount of crimson liquid onto the ground before her, her face paling. "Besides, I deserve this."

"No one deserves this," I tell her, sounding sincere, searching for any way to help her. I reach for her, and when I see the fear spark in her eyes, I stop my hand hanging midair.

"I am going to help you sit up," I calmly reassure her, gently easing her into a sitting position; with every little movement, she cries out in agony.

I kneel beside her, letting her use my body for support. She coughs up more blood into her hands as if she has just scooped up a handful of water; her bright green eyes meet mine, filled with acceptance and no hint of fear.

"Woah," I say when he drops the flashback. I glance around the training field before meeting his eyes. "It's worse than what I imagined. God, she's been through so much."

But she's become so strong.

"Yeah, she's been dealt a bad hand in her young life, which is why she has to accept the fact that she is immortal," Jay continues. "But in doing so, she has to accept the fact that she was raped and killed that night. If she doesn't, she won't ever awake her immortal abilities."

"But she can read minds, heal, and send thoughts," I comment, confused.

"Mind reading and healing is like a built-in system when you get turned. She doesn't take advantage of that; she tries to act like she is still a normal human, which isn't the case," he explains as he stares in the direction of the house as if trying to see her.

"How do we help her?"

"Unfortunately, we can't," he says, the disappointment obvious in his voice. "She has to overcome her fear and accept what happened that night, that the old her died then. She has to do this part herself."

"But she fights well," I comment, thinking he is reading too much into it, but part of me knows exactly what he is talking about. I have seen her freeze in front of Abe.

"As a human, she does fight well. But she could be so much better—almost unbeatable—if she accepted the harsh reality," he explains. "She could become stronger and faster. Every immortal has a unique ability, but it takes practice to control."

"So, once she overcomes her fear of Abe, she could become an undefeatable goddess?" I ask. "Kind of like Willow from *Buffy* when she gives all the chosen ones their abilities?"

"Taking a guess, you watched it with your mom? She loved that show," Jay asks; I nod my head in answer. "Yeah, basically. Minus a few things, considering Willow was a witch. But she can't keep hiding away from the truth.

"Rik, if she doesn't become her whole self before she kills, it will break her. And it's going to be difficult to get her back," he adds, worry in his eyes.

"What do you mean by that?" I ask, worried myself.

"The human part of Selen will feel overwhelming guilt. I have to admit, though, that she has come a long way from the girl I found on the road years ago. I think she is starting to accept it," he says, seemingly lost in his thoughts. "It's going to take time, and it has to be done on her own terms. But I know she will get through it. She is a fighter."

"Does she know any of this?"

"She knows most of it, but not the part about killing before she accepts. That would add more stress, and she is still fragile. I'm afraid it would break her mentally if she tries to accept the facts before she is ready," he says with a look of deep sorrow.

"I understand. I won't say anything. Hopefully, I can help her through it."

"I think you are already helping her by showing her what true love looks like. It is something she has never experienced before," Jay replies. "Speaking of which, you may want to head back and check on her. She always gets a little hard on herself."

"Yeah. I'll talk to you later."

I turn and head toward her house. I've learned much about this beautiful woman I'm lucky to call my girlfriend. No one should ever go through what she has, but here she is, still standing and trying to regain control of her life.

I walk onto the small back porch and open the door, stepping into the cool air that greets me, almost taking my breath away. I scan the kitchen and living room but find no Selen. *She must be upstairs.*

Sweet Vengeance

Walking up the stairs, I notice her art room door cracked open; I creep up to it. Inside, I find her in black jeans and a red crop top, dancing around with bright purple headphones on. Her short dark hair bounces slightly as she paints furiously onto the canvas, lost in her creativity.

I lean against the doorframe, watching in amazement.

Chapter 32

  I get lost in my painting, jamming out to my music and losing track of time. I add the final touches to the painting before me. Pulling back, I look at the finished artwork. The black background is starting to brighten in the center, almost like the glowing light of a fresh start. The skeleton before the bright light slowly rises, regaining its skin in patches along its bony structure. Arrows protrude from its body, though its bony hands are ripping them out. It's almost as if they are regaining their strength and starting to see the light at the end of the dark tunnel they have been trapped in, the light that will lead them to a better future. Roses sprout near its feet from a pool of blood, turning the darkness into beauty.

  Pulling off my headphones, I hear a soft shuffle sound behind me. Spinning around, I throw a blade; it stabs into the sheetrock by Rik's head, who happens to be standing against the door frame, his stormy-blue eyes staring at me.

  He glances at the blade and puts his hands up in surrender. "Woah, it's just me. I didn't mean to startle you."

Sweet Vengeance

"How long have you been standing there?" I ask him as I watch him reach up, tearing the blade out of the wall, then walk over to me. He hands me the knife to me, hilt first.

"A few minutes," he says, shrugging.

I slide the blade back into its place as he pulls me into his warm embrace. Leaning down, he presses a soft, loving kiss to my lips. The taste of honeysuckle floods my tastebuds. He pulls back and admires my freshly painted masterpiece.

"I love it. It's similar to the one I have, except this one looks like it's starting to accept and rebuild itself to a stronger version, into something beautiful," he comments, surprising me. "Almost like you."

"I guess something like that. I don't like to think too hard about what I'm painting," I admit. "I just lose myself in the music and let myself paint my feelings. I never know what it is until I finish."

"Well, they always turn out amazing," he says. "If you're done here, maybe we could watch a movie. If you are up for it?"

"Yeah, that sounds amazing. Let me add my signature and clean up. Then I'll be right down."

Rik nods, placing a kiss against my forehead before he heads downstairs. Grabbing an ultra-fine paintbrush, dip it in white paint and scribble *SSS* off to the skeleton's side.

Holding the used paintbrushes and tray, I walk to the bathroom and wash them until the water runs clear. As I step out, I return my art supplies to the room and lock the door behind me.

My phone dings. Pulling it out, I check the message, and a picture pops up on the screen, nearly taking my breath away. I lower myself to the floor, horrified as I read the message:

> WHAT MAKES HIM BETTER THAN ME? YOUR PARENTS KNOW YOU ARE ALIVE AND HIRED ALARIK TO TAKE YOU OUT, SINCE I FAILED....

The attached photo is of Rik in front of my parent's house, my dad handing him a bundle of cash. Tears start to run down my cheeks, my breathing coming in ragged gasps as I feel like I have just been punched in the gut. My heart pounds hard in my chest, the rush of blood flooding my ears.

I have the enemy under my roof.

My mind runs through every possibility. That night at the bar, I thought he was following Abe, but what if he was following me? Even though I was disguised, maybe he recognized me. Then, he also showed up at Abe's house and was looking for any reason to try to kill me. What if he planned to throw me off, then trick me into trusting him so he could do what he was hired to do? Is that why he invited someone he barely knew to stay at his house? It would be a clever move.

I thought he loved me. But now I wasn't sure.

Even if Rik was hired to take me out and still planned on it, I wouldn't give up that easily; I am no longer anyone's toy.

Sweet Vengeance

I pull myself off the floor and step into the bedroom, shutting the door silently behind me and creep to the bedroom window. Opening it, I crawl onto the roof as the sadness fades, replaced by anger. This all started with my hateful father.

I creep across the shingled roof to the edge and leap down, landing gracefully with a soft thud. I stand, glancing back at my house as darkness falls, the lights shining through the windows. Inside, Rik is sitting on the couch, glancing toward the stairs as he patiently waits for me. My chest feels like I have a gaping hole where my heart should be. The betrayal cuts deep, worse than the blade he shoved in my shoulder that night. I would rather take that blade over this blinding, unseen pain ripping through me.

Pulling my gaze away from my house, I walk into the woods, vanishing into the dark as I return to where it all started.

I find myself standing before my parent's house, where I grew up and was abused daily. The two-story cream-colored house stands tall as if taunting me. Its black shutters stand out against the exterior paint, the lights shining brightly through paper-thin curtains. Like a trail of breadcrumbs, all the abuse, rape, and betrayal lead back to the very place it all started.

I was around five, wearing a pretty white dress with multicolored flower designs. Mom was gardening, and I was playing in the soil, being a typical kid. Of course, my dress was covered in mud. My parents laughed as the neighbors walked by, smiling at the little girl playing in the front yard, having the time of her life.

When we returned inside, my parents were furious and punished me severely. I was whooped until my skin was broken and bleeding. Unable to sit, I was cruelly locked in my room without food.

Violet S.R. Cox

But no one knew those horrors. They were great at putting on a show in public, but behind closed doors, my parents became hideous, tormenting monsters.

"*Selen, where are you?*" Alarik's voice pops into my head, panicked, abruptly drawing me back to reality.

"*You can stop putting on a show. I know the truth. You were hired to kill me,*" I reply harshly through the bond; despite my anger, my heart shatters into a million pieces. "*We are through. Don't let me see you again, or you might regret it.*" I slam up the mental barrier against him when I finish. I don't want to hear any excuses or see him again.

I walk up the red brick sidewalk leading to the front door. The solid red door seems as scary as before, but I am not running away this time.

I raise my hand shakily and rap my knuckles against the sturdy wood. Anxiously, I wait for an answer; it feels like an eternity before the door creaks open, revealing my father's bony face, his ash blonde hair cut short and starting to gray. His cruel brown eyes go wide as his eyes land on me.

"Scarlett?" he asks, my old name sounding foreign to my ears.

"Hi, Dad," I reply, making my voice sound normal, trying to come off as if I don't know anything about them hiring two guys to kill me.

He opens the door wide as if welcoming me back and gestures for me to come in. I feel the fearful girl trying to surface as I step past the threshold into the house of my nightmares. I mentally shove my younger self into a cage, locking her inside me.

Sweet Vengeance

I am no longer afraid. It is time to confront them. I can't and won't live in fear any longer. I am no longer that weak, pathetic girl. I am no longer defenseless.

Looking around at the house, I see that it looks exactly the same, except there are no photos of me hanging on the wall anymore. It's as if I never existed.

My father leads the way into the living room, every step stiff, and he keeps glaring back at me as we walk through the hallway. As we step into the tan living room, I notice the same awful beige couch and recliner sitting there, along with the same old coffee table that I hit my back on, right in the same spot it was all those years ago. They haven't even bothered to rearrange. The only difference is there are photos sprawled on the walls of them on vacations, smiling like they have no regrets or care in the world.

"Honey, who was at the—" A soft gasp sound from the hallway.

Turning, I find my mom frozen in her place, and when her eyes land on me, her face whitens as if she has just seen a ghost. Her pale blonde hair is tied back into a ponytail, and her hazel eyes immediately look everywhere but at me.

"Hi, Mom," I greet her, smiling sweetly.

"Uh, hi, sweetheart," she mutters, trying to muster a smile.

"What is the matter, Mom? Are you not happy to see your daughter alive and well?"

"Uh, of course I am. We were worried sick about you," she says in a rush. "What happened? Where were you?" Though she tries to come off as a concerned, caring mother, I can sense the hint of disgust in her voice.

"Oh, stop the bullshit," I mutter as I walk to the couch and plop on it carelessly, glaring at both my parents.

"Excuse me?" my father practically shouts at me, his temper flaring up.

"You heard me," I say defiantly. He clenches his hands into fists by his side, his face turning red.

"What makes you think we weren't worried?" he demands.

I lean forward on the couch, tapping my finger on my temple as if trying to remember. "Oh, I don't know. Maybe it's the fact that you hired Abe to get rid of me."

"We never did—"

"Yes, you did! So cut the bullshit," I snap; his eyes go wide in surprise. "I know everything. I know that you hired Abe to get rid of me, and you hired Alarik when you found out I was alive."

Shock flashes across my parent's faces.

"Young lady, you need to leave. NOW!" my father sternly shouts, pointing toward the door.

"Nah, I think I'll stay a while." I lean back into the couch, crossing one leg over top of the other as my father reaches for his phone.

"I really hope you're calling the cops," I say as he dials. Then I can watch them put you in handcuffs."

Sweet Vengeance

He glances up at me, confused.

"Did you really think that I never took pictures of all the bruises you inflicted on me?" I ask him, arching an eyebrow in amusement. "Let's not mention the picture I have of you hiring a hitman and handing him money to kill me."

My father slowly puts his phone down, crossing his arms across his chest.

"You know all of this and yet decide to show your useless self here?" he asks harshly. The voice that used to terrify me is merely amusing now.

"Sure, why not?" I ask cheerfully, a smile on my face. I feel oddly calm as I stare my abusers in the eyes. "Cause, you see, I am not the same helpless girl I was two years ago. I have changed, I am stronger, and I am done dealing with the bullshit."

My father storms toward me, and I quickly stand up, ready to face him as he raises his hand. It comes speeding toward my face, but I stop his hand mid-air and bend his thumb back against his wrist, making him fall to his knees before me. I hear the gasp of horror escape my mother behind me as he looks up at me in surprise and pain, struggling to break my hold.

"Really? You thought you were going to get away with that again?" I ask, glaring down at this pathetic man before me. I chuckle, shaking my head at him. "The next time you raise a hand to me, you will find out just how cruel I can be." I release him and shove him back, stepping away as he stares at me in horror.

Suddenly, I fall forward onto all fours as a sharp pain explodes in my head. I glance up to find my mother behind me, holding a wooden bat and glaring down at me. Laughing, I pull myself off the floor; my mother stares at me in horror as I straighten, meeting her hazel eyes.

"Now, that wasn't very nice," I scold her.

"What the hell is wrong with you? Are you insane?" she asks, panicking as she backs away from me, the bat slipping from her hand and falling to the floor.

"As a matter of fact, yes, Mom. I am insane," I calmly tell her as another psychotic laugh escapes me.

A loud bang echoes through the house, causing me to jerk my head toward the front door.

Rik comes storming into the living room like he owns the place, his chest visibly rising and falling with anger as his eyes scan the room before coming to a stop on me. I can see the relief wash over him when he sees I'm uninjured.

What the hell is he doing here?

A laugh of insanity escapes past my lips as I look around the living room, my eyes landing first on my mother, then my father, and finally coming to a stop on Rik—the one who I thought loved me but was really out to kill me.

How stupid could I be? To think a guy like him wanted a girl like me...

"Looks like it's a party now," I say, gesturing around me. I feel myself slipping as I slowly lose hold of my sanity.

"Selen, what the hell is wrong with you?" Rik demands, his eyes full of concern as he watches me. I let out a howl of laughter, my eyes glued to his, shaking my head as if he just told the funniest joke.

"Nothing, this is the best I have ever felt," I reply.

Sweet Vengeance

    I see movement out of the corner of my eye and turn to look when I feel the stinging pain of a palm against my cheek; a blinding flash floods my vision momentarily as I fall to the ground.

    I look up to find my father looming over me.

CHAPTER 33
Alarik's POV

"Oh, Thank God. You showed up to take care of the problem," her father, who hired me, says as he hovers over Selen.

Red-hot anger rises within me as I stare down at the woman I love, now sporting a red handprint on her cheek. Stalking across the living room, my eyes are fixed on Selen, who looks up at me in betrayal, but I see no fear in her as she pulls herself off the ground.

"Yes, please do take care of his little problem," she sneers, glaring at me.

I stop before her and her father. Selen crosses her arms, shifting most of her weight onto one leg. I can't help but fixate on the red mark on her cheek. It enrages me.

Sweet Vengeance

I grab her father's throat and slam him against the closest wall. His hands immediately go to his throat as he tries desperately to break my hold; his face slowly turns red as he stares wide-eyed at me. I glance at Selen, who is watching us, confused, as her mother moves toward me. Pulling out a blade, I press it against her husband's throat, which causes her to halt in her tracks, horrified tears pour down her face.

"Please don't kill him. He didn't do anything wrong," Selen's mother begs.

"You move again, he dies," I tell her sternly, and she nods.

I return my gaze to Selen, who still stares at me in bewilderment, unsure if she can trust me. Peeling my eyes away from her, I look back to her father, wide-eyed and red-faced from the lack of oxygen. I release my hold on his throat, and he falls to the ground, gasping as he glares at me.

"I... hired you... to take care of her," he tells me, his voice sounding scratchy between coughing fits. The pathetic woman sidesteps me warily as she inches to tend to her husband. I back away, leaning against the wall that meets the one he was just pushed against, to where I can see both her parents and the woman I love.

"Yeah, you did. But you left out one crucial detail about my target."

"What?" he demands, glaring at me over his wife as she hugs him, burying her crying face into his shoulder.

"The fact that she's your *daughter*!" I snap.

"It shouldn't matter. I paid you!"

Violet S.R. Cox

"Actually, you paid me to take care of a stalker who was threatening your teenage daughter," I explain, pointing to Selen. "She *is* your daughter, and she is no stalker. Why would a father want his own daughter killed?"

"Hold up," Selen says, her hands palms facing out in the air as if gesturing to stop. She squints in confusion and tilts her head slightly. "You thought I was stalking his daughter but didn't know I *was* his daughter?"

"Yeah. He claimed that a stalker threatened his daughter and showed me a picture of you. He even provided threatening emails, which were obviously fake," I explain. She takes a slow step forward.

"So you didn't know the truth?" she asks, her voice small. I shake my head. "But how did you know it was me wearing the blonde wig?"

I feel the smile form as I stare into her eyes.

"I recognized those beautiful green eyes from the picture."

She smirks as she looks at the floor shyly and practically runs over to me, throwing her arms around my neck. I pull her body against mine, embracing her.

"Hold up a damn minute. You fell in love with this useless excuse of a human being?" her father demands.

I tense up at what he just called her. Selen pulls back out of my arms, turning to face her father.

"All she has ever done is ruin people's lives. Ever since the day she was born," he hisses.

Sweet Vengeance

I take a step toward him, pissed off. Selen puts her arm in front of me, gesturing for me to stop, and I do, glaring daggers at her father.

Selen steps forward and stands tall and stares her parents down.

"So, let me get this straight," she starts, which mildly perks my curiosity about what she is about to say. "Because two stupid teenagers decided to have unprotected sex like morons—oh, by the way, that's you—" she points at the two of them "—and get pregnant at the age of sixteen, it's somehow the baby's fault?

"I never forced you to have sex. It's not my fault that you didn't know what a condom was. For once in your life, take the fucking responsibility for your fuck ups. If you didn't want me, you could have put me up for adoption instead of blaming me for your mistake. Which everyone makes." She adds the last part softly.

That's my girl. I can't help but smirk as I lean against the wall, watching her tear them into a new one as her parents stare in complete shock at her finally standing up for herself.

"You need to respect your parents, young lady," her father says sternly as he slowly stands and takes a step toward her.

Uh oh. Bad choice, buddy. I observe at the ready if she needs me, but this is her fight, so I will not intervene.

A dark, humorous laugh sounds from her as she faces her father.

Oh this is going to be good.

"Parents? That's a fucking joke, right?"

"No, it's not a joke. And watch your language," he growls at her.

"That's a *fucking* joke and a half!" she snaps at him, purposefully emphasizing the cuss word. "You were never my parents; you were just my abusers. So *hell* to the *fucking* no. I will not show you any respect. You don't deserve it."

Her father raises his hand again; before I can stop him, Selen is pressing a blade against his throat. *Damn girl.* He freezes, putting both hands up in surrender, his face contorted with fear as their eyes lock.

"I warned you never to raise your hand to me again," she hisses as she shoves him back into the wall, hard enough to make his head bounce against it with a thump.

As I watch her take charge, I realize Jay is right: she will be unstoppable one day.

Chapter 34

I don't recognize my voice as it meets my ears. I'm focused on the man who abused me daily, pinned against the wall, with my dagger pressed against his throat. The man I once feared now stands before me, cowering in fear.

Funny how the tables have turned.

I hear a sudden move off to the side of me; glancing in the direction of the sound, I find my mother trying to sneak up on me with the bat in her hands again. Pulling the blade away from my father's throat, I spin, coming face to face with her.

As she swings it toward me, I block it with my forearm. The impact causes a brief pain before I snatch the bat from her and slam it over my knee, splitting it in two and tossing it to the floor. She throws herself at me, attacking me, or at least trying to, but each swing of her fist misses its target as I dodge or block it.

"Oops, you missed," I sarcastically comment, which enrages her more.

Violet S.R. Cox

"YOU UNGRATEFUL PIECE OF SHIT!"

A laugh escapes past my lips as I stare into her hazel eyes.

"No, not ungrateful. Just fed up," I state simply, "You have abused me and treated me like your own personal Cinderella. And no matter what the fuck I did, it was never good enough."

She swings her fist toward my face; I stop it mid-air and pull her closer, making her stare me in the eyes. Her eyes go wide as she realizes just how strong I am now.

"Why couldn't you just love me like any other mother would?" I ask, my voice almost broken.

I needed an answer.

"Have you really never figured it out?" my mom asks me with a smirk. She swings her other hand toward me, hoping she could catch me off guard, but to her shock, I grab her arm with my other hand, then head butt her in the face. I hear a crunching sound before she falls to the ground, groaning in pain as she wipes her hand under her now bleeding nose.

"What are you talking about?" I demand angrily.

"This is my chance. She is distracted." I hear my father's thoughts; he shuffles behind me.

My eyes land on Rik, leaning against the wall and watching the show. I feel a smile form, and he arches an eyebrow in curiosity. When my father wraps his arm around my throat and tightens, Rik pushes off the wall but stops when I shake my head.

"I got this."

He nods his head in understanding and leans back.

"Let me know if you need me."

My father pulls his arm back tighter, trying to cut off my supply of oxygen, but I bring my elbow back into his stomach, forcing him to release me. I spin, grabbing his outstretched arm, and kick him in the stomach, then flip him by his arm. He crashes onto the floor back-first with a loud thump, leaving him gasping for breath, glaring up at me. I glare back, shaking my head at him.

My mother stumbles to her feet behind me; turning, I pull out one of my throwing blades and let it loose. It bites angrily into her shoulder, making her fall back to the ground with a scream of agony. The blood seeps from the wound around the hilt, soaking her tan t-shirt.

My father's hand lands on my shoulder. With my dagger in my right hand, I spin to the left, arm outstretched before me, and feel the blade slice across the flesh of his throat—wet, hot blood splatters on my hand and arm.

"Selen, no." I hear Rik's voice in my head as I watch my father's brown eyes widen, and his hands fly to the gaping wound on his throat. As he tries to stop the bleeding, he falls to his knees. His eyes are glued to mine in fear as his life force flows freely.

The screams of terror from my mother echo through the house; she stares in horror, watching her husband die a gruesome death at her own daughter's hand.

Violet S.R. Cox

I feel the smile spread across my face when he finally falls to the ground, going still.

One down, two to go.

I stalk across the short distance to where my mother cowers, tears streaming down her bloody mess of a face, her nose crooked, probably broken from when I head-butted her. I kneel before her, gripping the hilt of my blade buried in her shoulder, ripping it out, causing her to scream in agony and making blood gush angrily from the wound. Returning the blade to its sheath, I spin the dagger I used only moments ago to murder my father in my hand.

"Please, Scarlett, I'm so sorry. Please don't kill me," she pleads. I meet her hazel eyes, overflowing with tears that mix with the blood smeared across her face.

"Scarlett died the night of prom," I state coldly. "And you know, I begged you every day for years to end the abuse. But lucky for you, I am feeling generous, Mother. So, if you can give me one good reason why I should show you the mercy that you could never show me, then maybe I will let you live."

My eyes are glued to hers as I play with the dagger caked in my father's blood, tapping it almost maniacally. She gulps as she stares nervously at the blade in my hand, trying to think of just one reason.

"Scarlett Selen Sirus," she starts, trying to sound stern with me, though her voice shakes. I arch an eyebrow in amusement. "Because I am your mom. Your one and only. You only get one."

I feel the smile form on my lips as I lower my head, chuckling as if she just told a joke before slowly returning my eyes to hers.

Sweet Vengeance

"As my mother," I air quote with my fingers, "it was your job to protect me, and you failed. So your reason is null and void," I state simply. "But don't worry, this will be quick compared to what you put me through over all those years." I press the tip of the dagger against her chest, over her heart; she whimpers in fear as the tears stream down her face faster.

Not taking my eyes off of hers, I shove the blade into her chest. I can feel her slowing heartbeat through the hilt as the fresh, warm blood rushes over it and onto my hand. Her hazel eyes widen once more before gradually falling shut.

As I pull out the blood-slicked blade, her body sags to the floor, motionless.

I stand up emotionless as I glance between the two dead bodies that used to be my parents, surrounded by growing pools of blood. I glance up at Rik, who stares at me in disbelief and worry as he studies me.

I place my dagger back in its sheath before walking into the kitchen, careful not to step in any of the blood. I grab a towel and a kitchen knife, careful not to touch them with my bare hands, before returning to the living room.

I walk over to my Mother's body first, bending and pushing the kitchen knife into the wound that killed her, then pulling it out. Then, I drag the sharp edge over the slash in my father's throat before placing the knife in his bloody hands. Standing, I wipe what I can of the blood on the kitchen towel and stuff it in my front pocket.

"What are you doing?" Rik asks, watching my every move. He jumps when I swipe my arm across the little table filled with photos of them, knocking them to the floor.

"She locked him out. He got pissed and kicked in the door. They got into an altercation. He grabbed a knife, stabbed her, then slit his own throat," I explain numbly, pointing between the two bodies.

"You've watched way too many crime shows," he comments as he slams his elbow back into the sheetrock, leaving a hole, adding to the evidence; a few hung photos fall to the floor after the impact.

"At least, it comes in handy," I tell him as I walk toward the front door, swiping pictures and lamps out of their places.

"Remind me never to piss you off to this point," he says, following me to the front door. The frame is splintered from being kicked in and is tilted on its hinges.

"Let's get out of here," I suggest as we walk out into the dark, scanning our surroundings and making sure no one sees us.

Rik picks up the pace, leading the way to his dark car parked down the street. We walk in utter silence.

"Get in," he says as he goes to the driver's side.

"Open the door," I say; he looks over the car at me, confused. *"So I don't leave any traces of blood on your car,"* I explain mentally. He nods and darts over, opening the door for me and then closing it behind me.

"Smart thinking," he says as he slides into the driver's seat, pulling away from the curb.

Sweet Vengeance

I keep my hands in my lap, careful not to touch anything in his car as he drives us back to my house. I feel oddly calm and cold, without remorse or a hint of guilt.

Maybe I have lost my sanity after all.

"How did you know where I was?" I question, my eyes landing on him. He takes his eyes away from the road for a moment, looking worried.

"I put myself in your shoes. Then I searched your old name, and your old address popped up," he explains. "How are you feeling?" he asks me, his voice concerned as we pull onto my dirt road.

"Believe it or not, strangely calm," I tell him honestly.

Two down, one to go!

Rik pulls into my driveway, and we go through the same routine to get out of the car.

"I need matches, and the hose," I tell him, walking over to the small burn pit.

I start stripping out of my bloody clothes, tossing them piece by piece onto the old ash. Rik walks back with the uncoiled hose as I pull my shoes and socks off, dropping them with the rest of the clothing before turning toward him in nothing but my black underwear and bra. He silently admires the sight of my body as he holds out the hose for me, setting my weapons on the ground. I scrub the dried, caked blood off my forearm and hands the best I can.

Is there any other evidence that has to be burned?

Violet S.R. Cox

"Do you have matches?" I ask as I pull away from the stream of water.

"Yeah. Give me a second," he answers, running back to his car.

I walk to the side of the house, grab a small gas can that I kept around for lawn care purposes, and turn the water off. Walking back to the fire pit, I tip the can and pour the gas onto the bloody pile of clothes, the stench of it burning my nostrils.

Rik's footsteps sound behind me as he returns. He trades me the matches for the gas can and steps back as I strike the match against the strip on the side, igniting it. I stare at the dancing flame for a second before I flip it into the pile of gas-drenched clothing. With a sudden whoosh and orange flare, I watch the clothes burn as the flames devour them.

Rik steps up beside me, handing me a black t-shirt that looks like one of his.

"Thank you," I say, slipping it on. I sit by the fire in one of the lawn chairs, watching the flames hungrily devour the evidence.

"You've put a lot of thought into this," he comments as he drags a chair beside mine and sits. "Are you okay?"

"Yeah, been planning this every day for the last two years. The only thing I have left besides a shower is to clean my weapons of any trace of evidence," I explain numbly, going through my mental checklist as I return my eyes to the flames dancing before me in the darkness.

"Are you sure you are okay? You're crying, babe," he says, the weight of his gaze forcing me to meet it.

Sweet Vengeance

Reaching up my hand to my cheek, I feel the moist trail of tears. I am surprised to wipe them away, chuckling and shaking my head.

"Two down, one to go," I say, my hand shaking as I pull it away from my face. My stomach harshly twists into knots, making me nauseous. "I never thought I would have to turn into this. Never thought I would have to kill my parents and become a monster. But, at least two-thirds of the problem is gone."

I stand up, pushing away any of the guilt that is trying to surface. Rik gets up and pulls me into a hug. I lay my head against his chest in silence, taking in the comfort of his earthy smell and the feel of his chest rising and slowly falling beneath my cheek.

"How about you go get a shower, and I'll clean your blades for you," he suggests as the fire dies out, leaving no trace of the bloody fabric behind. Nodding my head in agreement, he bends, grabbing my daggers from the ground where I set them earlier, and we head inside. I head upstairs to the shower while he heads to the kitchen with the bloody weapons.

Standing under the scalding hot shower, I scrub every inch of my skin until it's red before getting out. I dry off most of the way before wrapping the towel around me and stepping out of the steamed-filled bathroom to find Rik sitting outside my bedroom door. He glances up at me when he hears the door open.

"Hey, sorry. I didn't want you running away again," he says, meeting my eyes as he stands. I walk past him into my room toward my dresser, and he adds, "We need to talk."

"Yes, we do," I say, swallowing past the lump in my throat. I glance up from the dresser drawer that I just opened, meeting Rik's gaze. "Why didn't you tell me that my father hired you?" He glances away guilty before his eyes return to mine.

"I should have. But that night at the bar, I realized that you weren't a stalker; even with that blonde disguise, I could see it in your gorgeous green eyes," he begins. "They told a whole different story in them, and I could see something much deeper than the bullshit your father tried to feed me. I could see the hurt and trauma. I wasn't certain until you cringed away from Abe when he came close to you.

"And when we fought, I realized you were trained, which intrigued me. What stalker knows how to fight? So, as time passed, I became very interested in you and slowly started falling in love with you. I never knew he was your father. He never told me his name or yours. He just gave me your picture and an email address."

"You grew interested in me?" I ask, feeling a smile form on my face. He smiles and nods.

"But, how did you find out?" he asks.

I look away, guilty. Grabbing my cell phone off the dresser, I pull up the text from Abe and hand my phone to him as I stare at the floor.

"If he didn't send a picture, I probably wouldn't have believed it. I thought you were the enemy; you were in the house, and I just had to escape. I am head over heels in love with you, and I don't want to kill you. It nearly killed me just thinking you were the enemy, Rik." I confess, tears streaming down my face as my eyes meet his stormy-blue ones. "I'm sorry I just disappeared like that. I should have come to you, but I didn't know what you would have done if I accused you. I don't want to kill the only guy who has ever shown me so much kindness."

As I step toward him, he drops the phone. His hands go to the sides of my face, thumbs wiping the tears away as his tongue runs over my bottom lip, sending a shiver through my body as he kisses me softly.

"Don't ever be sorry for your survival instincts," he says, pulling back from my lips, his forehead pressed against mine. I nod in understanding, biting my lower lip. "Don't do that," he growls lowly, tempted. "Do you realize what that does to me?"

He steps back to look at me, and I smirk, shaking my head. His gaze takes on a dark edge of temptation as he scans my nearly naked body.

"Please, do tell me, though." I seductively say as I step forward, purposefully biting my lower lip and looking him in the eyes.

"Selen," he half moans as he eyes me. "You are driving me nuts. God, you look fucking sexy. All I want to do to you when you do that is—"

"So do it."

I let the towel slip, leaving me standing naked before him. I close the distance between us, my lips landing on his hungrily as the sweet flavor of honeysuckle floods my taste buds.

Chapter 35

Rik's intoxicating earthy aroma surrounds me as the sweet taste of honeysuckles washes over me, making me crave more of those sweet lips on mine. His arms wrap around me, pulling me tightly against his clothed body. Our lips clash in a frenzy, his hands traveling my curves, leaving warm tingles blossoming behind in their wake. My heart beats rapidly in my chest with the need to be satisfied.

I pull away as my hands find the end of his shirt and tug it off, exposing his perfectly tanned muscular chest. He yanks it the rest of the way over his head and lets it drop silently to the floor, eyeing me with a new hunger.

He pulls me against him, our bare torsos touching, sending me ablaze from the skin-on-skin contact. As his lips land on mine again, my hands travel every inch of his body, only stopping on the button of his jeans. I fumble to unfasten his pants, his intoxicating kisses making it impossible to think as I melt further into him. Slowly, I manage it, pushing his pants down, and Rik briefly breaks the kiss, pulling them off the rest of the way. His lips crash back against mine as his arms wrap around my waist, pulling me flush against him, and a new burst of heat engulfs me.

"Rik." I pull back breathlessly, peeking up at him nervously. "I want to do something to satisfy you for a change," I say shyly.

Surprises pass over his face, soon replaced with confusion. I slowly kneel before him, sliding his boxers down and off. *Damn, he's huge. I'll never get used to this reveal.* I look nervously up at Rik, who is watching my every move.

"Selen, you don't have to."

"I know I don't have to, but I want to," I tell him, quickly adding, "And you have to remember that I am still kind of new at this."

I part my lips and take him into my mouth.

Rik catches his breath as I bob my head back and forth, taking his entire length until I gag, making tears spring into the corner of my eyes. Soft moans of pleasure escape him as his hand lands on the back of my head gently, carefully moving my mouth at a pace he likes. A throbbing desire rushes into me as the wetness slowly builds between my legs.

Pulling him out of my mouth, I stand and kiss him, gently backing him up to the bed. With his knees on the edge of the mattress, he falls back; I crawl over him, straddling his hips, earning a curious look from him as he studies the view. Lifting my hips, I grab him and guide him into me.

Lowering myself onto him, his massive length enters me, filling me with a brief painful bliss as I arch my back, slowly moving my hips against him as I ride him, bliss flooding my body—the pressure begins to build in my core, eager for sweet release.

Rik grabs my hips as he meets my hips halfway with his thrusts. His hands glide over my stomach up to my breast, cupping them and gently pinching my nipples, sending a blissful spasm bursting through my body. Our soft moans surround us as our body heat combines, engulfing us, almost suffocating us as we lose ourselves in bliss.

"Fuck," Rik groans out loud as another spasm spreads like wildfire through my body. Pushing myself down onto him, clinging to him like a second tattoo, I pant hard as I grab the covers into my fist behind his head.

Rik holds my thigh and rolls over on top of me, still deep inside. He pulls out of me, leaving me craving more of his length as he stands. Grabbing my hips, he pulls me to the edge of the bed, placing my legs on his massive shoulders. He levels himself at my entrance, where I impatiently await him to become one with me again.

He slides his hand down my leg to my thigh, teasing me, before grabbing his length and pushing himself deep inside me, making me gasp in pleasure as he enters. His hands grip my hips as he deepens his thrusts, making me bite my lower lip, trying to suppress the moans as the pressure builds. I hear him half growl, and as I look up, I see him eyeing my lip as a new profound look of lust takes him, and he thrusts harder.

"You are driving me crazy," he pants, quickening his pace as his hand slides up to my breast, cupping it while pounding deep within me. The pressure building is almost unbearable, bringing me to the verge of screaming.

Sweet Vengeance

I feel when he nears his climax; on the brink of an orgasm, he pulls himself out abruptly and lies on the bed. "Crawl back on top," he instructs between pants.

Desperate for release, I roll over and straddle his hips with shaky legs. He guides his shaft into me this time as I lower myself and grind against his hips, pushing him in and out of me. I feel the pressure building up again as he grabs my hips and starts moving with me as I lean my head back, arching into his thrusts, moans escaping past my lips with every spasm and bringing me closer to the brink of an orgasm that I know is coming.

Rik swells within me as I grind harder and faster, and soon, I feel his sweet release, followed by the earth-trembling orgasm that floods my body. Our loud moans create an incredible mashup as they mix.

I nearly collapse on top of him, panting and lightheaded. Rik's fingers stroke my back softly, almost putting me asleep on top of him as I regain my breathing. Sitting up, unsure if my legs will properly work, I carefully remove him from me, feeling the disappointing empty void, and lay down next to him.

"Why does it feel like the first time with you every time?" I ask breathlessly, meeting his stormy-blue eyes. He smiles as he turns, lying on his side.

"I don't know. I was about to ask you the same thing," he says as he moves one of the short strands of my hair out of my face.

I stand up and stagger to the dresser on my wobbly legs, feeling like I'm on a boat. I hear Rik chuckling as he grabs his clothing. Holding my change of clothes, I return to the bed, and after getting dressed, I curl up under the covers with Rik.

Violet S.R. Cox

He pulls me close against him and kisses me softly before I drift off into the darkness of sleep.

Sweet Vengeance

CHAPTER 36

My father's brown eyes widen, and his hands fly to the gaping wound on his throat. As he tries to stop the bleeding, he falls to his knees. His eyes are glued to mine in fear as his life force flows freely. The screams of horror from my Mother echo through the house; glancing back at her, I watch as she stares in horror, watching her husband die a gruesome death at her daughter's hand.

I stalk across the short distance to where my Mother is cowering, tears streaming down her bloody mess of face, her nose crooked. I kneel before her, gripping the hilt of my blade buried in her shoulder, ripping it out, causing her to scream in agony and make blood gush angrily from the wound.

"Please, Scarlett, I am sorry. Please don't kill me." she pleads, begging me for mercy. I meet her hazel eyes, tears flowing from them as she pleads for her life, the tears mixing with the blood smeared across her face.

"Scarlett died the night of prom." I state coldly. "And you know, I begged y'all everyday for years to end the abuse. But lucky for you I am feeling *generous Mother. So, if you can give me one good reason why I should show you mercy that you could never show me, then maybe I will let you live."* I tell her, my eyes glued on hers as I play with my Father's blood that cakes the dagger as I tap it playfully almost maniacally. I watch my Mom gulp as she stares nervously at the bloody dagger in my hand and tries to think of just one reason.

"Scarlett Selen Sirus," she starts trying to sound stern with me. I arch an eyebrow in amusement. *" Because I am your Mom. Your one and only. You only get one."* she tells me, her voice shaking. I feel the smile form on my lips as I lower my head shaking, chuckling as if she just told a joke, before slowly returning my eyes to hers.

"As my Mother," I air quote with my fingers. *"It was your job to protect me and you failed. So your reason is null and void."* I state simply. *"But don't worry, this will be quick compared to what y'all put me through over all those years."* I add pressing the tip of the dagger against her chest, over her heart, she whimpers in fear as the tears stream down her face faster.

Not taking my eyes off of hers, I shove the blade into her chest; I can feel her slowing heartbeat through the hilt; as the fresh warm blood rushes over it and onto my hand. Her hazel eyes widen once more before shutting. I stare at my hands, soaked in the red, warm slippery liquid, almost like melted butter.

I suddenly wake from the nightmare. My heart is pounding, and I'm drenched in sweat, the shock leaving my stomach twisted in knots. I look down at my hands in the dark and swear I can see blood still staining them; blinking, my hands are clean again.

I glance over at Rik, who is in a deep sleep, and slowly get out of bed, careful not to wake him. Going downstairs, I round the corner and come face to face with my father, a red gash across his throat—the wound I inflicted. I clamp my hand over my mouth, suppressing a scream of horror. The sound of my heartbeat floods my ears, and I shut my eyes, trying to slow my breathing and calm myself.

When I open my eyes, I find only empty space before me.

I scan the living room, searching for movement, trying to figure out what is happening. I know they are dead, but I feel the cold whisper of dread wash over me like a cold shower. I don't find anything.

Nice, Selen. You're really going insane now.

Walking into the kitchen, my eyes dart around the room as I approach the fridge, take water out, and slowly relax. As I close the fridge door and turn around, I find my mother standing before me, whimpering, begging me not to kill her, with tears running down her face. Glancing down, I see my hand on a blade plunged into her chest, blood pooling around it and coating my hand in its crimson fury.

Fear slams into me as the water bottle slips from my hand, landing with a soft thud on the kitchen floor and momentarily grabbing my attention. When I look up again, my mother is gone. I stumble away, my back hitting the fridge as tears streak my cheeks.

What the hell is happening?

"Jay, are you awake? I need you," I mentally ask as my heart beats loudly in my chest. I scan my surroundings in terror.

"Selen, what's wrong? I can feel your fear. I am on the way," Jay's worried voice fills my head.

Violet S.R. Cox

"I... I think I'm going crazy," I send back as I slowly slide down the fridge to the kitchen floor, drawing my knees up to my chest, eyes darting all around me.

I jump at the sound of the back door opening, jerking my head up to find Jay walking in. His worried eyes immediately land on me, and he rushes over me. His hair falls free to his shoulders untamed, and he is dressed in blue flannel pajama pants and a plain black t-shirt. Worriedly, he scans my body for injuries, but finds none.

"Selen, where is Rik?" he asks, concerned.

"He's asleep. I don't want to worry him. I think I've scared him enough," I mutter as I eye my surroundings. My gaze stops behind Jay, on my father, who is standing there, blood gushing from the slit on his throat, eyes wide.

Jay quickly looks behind him and then returns his eyes to me, confused. "What is it?"

"You... d-don't see him?" I hear myself stuttering badly with fear.

"No, there is no one there," he reassures me; despite his words, I glance at him and then back at the empty spot where my father was just standing.

"Selen, what is going on?" he asks, worry masking his face as he tries to stay calm.

"I... I keep seeing my parents," I choke through the tears that are soaking my face.

Sweet Vengeance

"Well, they did abuse you," he says, his expression relaxing slightly in understanding. "Maybe you think they are searching for you."

Suddenly, I realize we never told him.

"No, I... I know for a fact that they aren't coming for me." I gulp, meeting his eyes. "I... I... I—" I can't stop stuttering as the sob escapes me.

"She killed them last night."

I jerk my head up at the sound of Rik's voice; he's standing behind Jay, wearing only his jeans, with his expression worried and confused as he looks at me. His bare chest has me staring for a few moments, lost in the memory of our shared blissful night.

In a flash of movement over his shoulder, I see my mother dripping blood on the floor as she walks up next to him. I gasp and drop my head in my hands—I must be going crazy.

I hear Rik walk toward me, kneeling at my side.

"She killed them?" Jay asks, surprised.

"Yeah," Rik confirms. "You trained her well."

I glance up, scanning the surroundings, before I find them both staring at me.

"It sounds like you may be experiencing guilt," Jay softly tells me. "Show me what you are seeing."

"Me too. I'm here to help," Rik adds as he softly rubs my shoulder, his touch chasing the coldness away. I feel the fear start to disperse as relief washes over me.

Taking both of their hands in my own and closing my eyes, I concentrate on the dream. As the recap finishes, I drop their hands and slowly open my eyes to find both of them studying me, their eyes filled with concern.

"You are experiencing guilt," Jay explains. "It's going to take time to fully accept what you have done. They're going to haunt you for a little bit."

"But why is the guilt just hitting her now?" Rik asks Jay as he stands, extending his hand to me and helping me to my feet.

"The adrenaline has worn off," Jay says. "You must learn how to block it, almost like when you don't want anyone in your head. Just redirect it toward the guilt." I nod in understanding. "Try to get some more rest. You're going to need it."

"Thank you," I whisper as I scan the house nervously. Rik pulls me into a hug, and I see Jay give him a questioning look as if asking if he had things handled from here. Rik nods against my shoulder, and I watch Jay leave.

"Why didn't you wake me?" Rik asks softly.

"You were sleeping so deeply, and I didn't want to worry you," I admit, looking down at the floor. I feel his finger under my chin, lifting my face to look at him.

"Your problems are also my problems. You should have woken me. We will battle your demons together," he says as he places a kiss on my forehead.

"Now, let's try to get some more rest," he adds, grabbing my hand and leading me back up the stairs to bed.

Violet S.R. Cox

CHAPTER 37
Alarik's POV

With every passing day, I watch as Selen battles her guilt, the demons of her past threatening to tear her apart. Her lifeless parents haunt her even in their deaths, and only she can see them. Her eyes constantly scan her surroundings as if she is in the middle of a battlefield, being hunted, and sometimes, she screams when she lets her guard down—washing her hands every few minutes as if trying to clean the invisible blood away.

She always wakes up crying.

It's now her fifth day battling her guilt, and we are watching a movie on the couch. She is curled up against me with her head on my shoulder, seemingly lost in her thoughts as she stares blankly at the television.

Sitting up suddenly and leaning forward, she closes her eyes as if concentrating on something mentally. Takes a deep breath and slowly exhales. When those beautiful eyes open again, I swear I see a new person take over as the strength and determination refill her, shining bright in her eyes. I realize she has won the mental battle against herself. Standing up, she turns, looking at me.

Uh oh.

"We need to get back to training," she states, almost like she is fully recharged and back to a hundred percent battery.

"Tomorrow. You still need to recuperate," I say, which earns me a look from her. *Oh, great. She's even more stubborn than before, as if she wasn't a handful to begin with.*

"I'm going to the training field with or without you. Doesn't matter to me. I wasted enough time sitting around here moping around," she says, and I can hear the new motivation in her voice. "I have one more job to take care of," she adds, pulling on her sneakers and heading to the backdoor.

I was right. She is going to be a lot more stubborn now.

Sighing, I push myself off the couch and follow her to the training field. She walks with a newfound confidence, but I can see she is thinking hard about something by the way she bites the corner of her lip.

When she arrives at the field, she walks over to the punching bag, eyeing it as if sizing it up; swinging her fist, she hits it, then spins around and kicks her leg out, knocking it sideways from the force. Her eyes keep glancing over at me as she bites the inside of her lip.

Shit. I know I'm not going to like what she's thinking.

Returning her attention to the punching bag, she hits it again, and the bag sways away from her from the impact of her fist.

"What's on your mind?" I ask, leaning against one of the trees closest to her. "And why do I get the feeling that I won't like it?"

She falls silent momentarily as she lets loose a punch and a kick before suddenly stopping and walking toward me with newfound energy; her approach is almost seductive.

"Because you aren't. You're going to hate it," she says, meeting my eyes before glancing away to the training field.

"Just tell me. I can tell by the way you won't look at me that it's most likely a very bad idea, too."

Taking a deep breath, her bright green eyes meet mine. Instead of telling me, she shows me the plan.

"Absolutely not. That is not happening," I tell her sternly, pissed at her for even thinking about doing that.

Chapter 38

From my place on the park bench beneath a single light post, I feel the tears running down my face. I never thought I would turn to my enemy or look for him. But maybe he isn't half the monster I thought he was.

The tears are still flowing when he arrives. Abe approaches with caution, making sure I'm not going to attack him again. Wiping the tears away with the back of my hand, he stops before me. I look up at him, the dark, starry night sky surrounding him.

"Why did you want to meet?" he asks me, his chocolate eyes watching me with what looks like concern, something I've never seen in them before.

I sweep my hands through my hair, pushing it back out of my face as I meet his eyes.

Violet S.R. Cox

"Why do you like me? Like out of all the girls, why me?" I ask him. He seems taken aback by my question and quickly scans the park as if searching for Rik.

"You are beautiful and always have been. You play hard to get while the other girls throw themselves at me. And I thought that was worth trying to get your attention. So, when your dad asked me to take you out, I couldn't pass up the offer," he starts as he crouches in front of me. "But why are you here asking me and not Alarik?" He studies me curiously as he asks the question, and my tears start again as I look down at my shaking hands.

"We... well... he broke up with me," I confess, meeting his eyes for a moment before my heart shatters into a million pieces. Surprise passes over his face for a split second, and I look at the ground.

"Why did he break up with you?" he asks as he puts a finger under my chin, slowly lifting my face until I look into his chocolate-brown eyes. He wipes away the tears with his thumb.

"He... He said he had... enough," I sob. "Because I couldn't get you out of my mind." He stares into my eyes, shocked, as he tries to process the information I just told him.

"Really? I thought you hated me for what I did to you," he says as he removes his hand from under my chin, gently brushing my chin-length hair behind my ear. His palm comes to rest against my face, and his thumb strokes my cheek softly. He studies me like he is lost in thought.

Embarrassed, I look away from his eyes and at the ground.

Sweet Vengeance

"No. You were my first love, and I will always love you. I hated myself for liking it, and I tried to put the blame on you. I shouldn't have run from you."

"So, you don't hate me?" he asks; I shake my head. "So, why exactly am I here, though?"

"I was wondering if you were up for it. Maybe... we could try to start over," I explain, fidgeting with my hands and refusing to look him in the eye. "You know me better than anyone else. That and I don't have anyone else to turn to."

He sits down on the bench beside me, silent.

"I'll understand if you don't want to," I continue. "I haven't exactly given you a reason to trust me." I turn to face him, meeting his eyes. He studies me as he mentally runs through all I have told him.

"I don't see why we can't give it another shot. I would love nothing more than to get to know you more," he says, his hand resting on my cheek, his thumb stroking my skin as he stares into my eyes. He leans forward and presses his lips against mine softly.

"Are you comfortable going back to my house?" he asks, pulling back to look at me.

I nod as he stands, extending his hand to me. I take it, and we walk hand in hand to his truck. I lean on his muscular shoulder as we walk across the gravel to this truck.

"Maybe I can show you a thing or two," I say as he opens the door for me. I crawl up inside and slide across to the passenger seat.

"Hm. I like the sound of that," he says, smiling excitedly as he climbs into the driver seat, turning the key; the engine sputters to life. He glances over at me before pulling out of the parking lot.

I scoot over to the middle seat, catching his attention as he drives. My hand goes to his inner thigh, surprising him. I run my hand from his thigh to his chest as he focuses on the road. I lean in, kiss his neck, and gently bite it. His breath hitches, and I know I must be driving him crazy. Running my lips over his neck up to his ear, I nibble on his skin softly before I sit back in my seat, my hand returning to his inner thigh, squeezing it gently as he pulls into his driveway.

When he puts the truck into park, he immediately turns to me.

Pulling me to him, he presses his mouth hungrily against mine, and my lips move against him as I wrap my arms behind his neck. He leaves trails of soft kisses from my lips down to my neck, where he playfully bites.

Reluctantly, he pulls back, opens the truck door, and slides out, extending his hand to me and helping me out.

How did I forget just how much of a gentleman he was? How sweet he was. That's why I fell for him in the first place.

Walking in the front door, I press him against the wall, kissing him furiously, taking him by surprise as he stands momentarily stunned before I feel his hands exploring my every curve. He lifts me with ease, and I wrap my legs around his waist, my arms looped over his shoulders as he carries me to his bedroom without breaking the kiss.

Gently, Abe lays me down on his bed before he pulls back, both of us panting as he pulls his shirt off, exposing his hard, muscular chest. He crawls onto

Sweet Vengeance

the bed, his legs on either side of me as he makes his way to my lips, kissing me again. His fingers find the hem of my shirt, and he doesn't rush as he takes his time before lifting it. The cool air kisses my exposed skin as his bare hand brushes against my flesh, sending shivers through me. He tugs off my shirt, exposing me in my black lace bra. Dropping the shirt on the bed beside me, he admires me, his eyes full of lust. Shyly, I look away.

"Get the fuck off her."

Alarik's voice fills the room. Looking up at Abe, I notice the blade pressed against his throat. I sit up and grab my shirt, hastily pulling it on as Rik stares at me in disbelief. Abe fearfully backs up to the wall.

"What the hell are you doing?" I demand as I stand up off the bed.

Rik looks back at me, anger tainting his features, staring at me as if I'd lost my mind. His stormy-blue eyes are grayer now as he looks between Abe and me.

"I break up with you, and you run back to your rapist. To the guy who tried to kill you!"

"Because I am more of a man than you," Abe says.

The laughter escapes past my lips, surprising me. I know Alarik won't hurt me, and well, Abe, he really fell for my charades.

I stalk over to where Rik has Abe pressed against the wall with the blade against his neck. Abe's eyes never leave me as he tries to figure out why I'm laughing maniacally.

Violet S.R. Cox

I'm going to enjoy this.

I press my shoulder against the cold wall next to Abe, studying him carefully, unable to stop the smile creeping across my face.

"If you guys broke up, then why the fuck are you here?" Abe demands, glaring at Rik, who glances over at me. I can see the hurt in his eyes, almost like a betrayal, making my heart drop. I look away; I can't afford the distraction right now.

I have to focus on my task.

"Yeah, Rik. Why did you follow me here?" I ask, mocking Abe, who shoots a glare at me.

"Because I don't want you to do anything that you may regret later. Believe it or not, I do love you," Alarik protests. "And like I told you, your battles are my battles. We do this together. So, I won't let you put your life in danger." Rik tells me, glancing over at me occasionally.

I push myself off the wall and stop beside Rik, facing Abe, who glares at me as he slowly pieces it together.

"Hold up. Did you really think she was going—" Rik starts as a chuckle escapes his lips. I stand on my tiptoes and press a quick kiss against Rik's lips before returning my attention to the pissed-off Abe.

"You played me?" he asks me in bewilderment as anger creeps into his tone. His chocolate brown eyes meet mine in disbelief as betrayal and hurt pass through them, clouded by intense anger.

Sweet Vengeance

"Did you really think I would return to you after you raped me?" I question as I glance over at Rik, who is smirking. "I think I missed my calling. I did some excellent acting. What are your thoughts?" I ask, my eyes landing on Abe, who is fuming. I swear I can see steam coming from his ears as he visibly shakes in anger.

"I think you deserve a reward," Rik comments.

Abe's chest is heaving as he tries to calm himself, his eyes fixed on me, going dark.

"You fucking bitch," he snarls as he lunges forward, pushing Rik's arm away and punching him, sending him to the ground. Abe steps over him and stalks toward me. "Now, you're really going to die," he growls as he backs me against the wall. "Not so tough now, are you?"

I look up at him, smiling as I once again let him think he has won. His hand wraps around my throat—his favorite move. Bringing my arm straight up, I twist my body to the side, slamming my elbow onto his outstretched arm, breaking his hold on me. Surprise flashes in his eyes as I shove him back, making him stagger, and he regains his footing.

"I am stronger now, and I'm done fearing you, you fucking bastard," I tell him calmly as I reach into my boot, pulling out my dagger. His eyes land on the steel nervously. I never thought this monster could show emotion, but I have seen him go through every emotion humanly possible as fear flashes in his eyes for a split second. Out of the corner of my eye, I see Rik standing as Abe lunges for me again.

Sidestepping his attack, he runs into the wall behind me, putting a hole in the sheetrock. He turns and runs at me again, letting out a growl of annoyance. I'm about to dodge again when he stops. I feel the stinging pain against my cheek as his palm meets my skin, sending me to the floor and causing tears to well up in my eyes as my vision blurs momentarily.

Looking up, I find Alarik standing between us, defending me; he lands a few good punches before Abe regains his composure and grabs Rik by his outstretched arm; he pulls him closer, then shoves him to the side, with a force that sends Rik rolling across the floor.

Abe's eyes land on me as I stand more determined than ever. I see Rik silently stand up and slowly creep up behind Abe, careful not to make any noise.

"Like we practiced."

Abe stalks toward me without paying Rik any attention—a deadly mistake.

Smiling, I watch as Rik grabs Abe's arms, pulling them behind him and kicking him in the back of the knee, forcing Abe to his knees before me. Abe stares at me as I stroll up to him; I kneel so I'm at eye level with him, his dark brown eyes only getting darker with rage.

"I never wanted to become this person, but you," I point at him with the tip of one of my daggers, "you are the monster that turned me into this when you took my innocence that night. When you took advantage of me, you thought my innocence was weakness." I admire my blade, my fingers dancing over it as I eye him, the panic obvious on his face as he struggles against Rik's hold. "Oh, don't worry, darling. I won't make you suffer the way you made me suffer."

"Let him break free."

Sweet Vengeance

"No. He could hurt you," Rik's voice sounds in my head.

"I will not kill a defenseless man. Let him think he broke free." I stand up and back away. *"I'll be fine."*

"Fine."

Abe breaks free from Rik, shooting to his feet, and rushes toward me. He tackles me to the floor; prepared for this move, I fall back and shove him over my head. He lands flat on his back. I jump from the ground and spin toward him, watching as he gasps for breath. He pulls himself off the floor and stalks toward me again. I run at him and swing my fist across his face, making his head snap to the side, then bring my hand back with the dagger.

I slam it deep in his throat.

Abe's eyes widen as blood pumps freely over my hand, covering the blade in its warmth. Readjusting my grip, I rip it out of his neck, and blood sprays from the wound, covering me in its red heat.

Abe falls to his knee and onto his side, his life force pooling around him as he chokes on his blood. I watch as the life drains from his eyes, and his head sags to the floor. The carpet is drenched crimson, and the bed and surrounding objects are now decorated in splashes of red.

Rik is standing before me; his lips are moving, but I can't hear what he is saying. Silence surrounds me as I stare at Abe's lifeless body sprawled in a pool of blood. I stare down at my hands, stained red, holding the murder weapon.

I actually did it.

"Selen, we have to go. Now." I finally hear Rik's voice as the world comes rushing back to me.

Grabbing me by the arm, he drags me out of the crime scene, snapping me out of my thoughts. I gather my bearings and snap into action, moving without being dragged.

We rush out of the house to his car, hidden in night's darkness. Opening the passenger door for me, I slide onto the leather seats as he shuts the door behind me and rushes to the driver's side.

My eyes are glued to Abe's house. I see a shadow move off to the corner, but it's gone within a second—most likely just a raccoon or my mind playing tricks on me. I search for any sign of movement but find nothing.

Rik plops into the driver seat, turns the key, and speeds off.

"Are you okay?" Rik asks, making me jump as he breaks the tense silence filling the car. I glance at the man beside me, who has helped me through everything. Without him, none of this would have been possible.

"Yeah, I believe so," I say as he drives. I notice he is doing the speed limit for once. "Are you?" I ask, arching an eyebrow at him.

"Yeah. I'm fine. I'm not the one covered in blood."

Looking down at myself, I find my clothes drenched in it. My stomach twists harshly, and the nausea hits just as Alarik pulls onto the dark dirt road.

"Pull over," I say as the nausea worsens. I feel on the verge of throwing up. He looks at me questionably, pulling off to the side. "I'm going—"

Sweet Vengeance

Before I finish the sentence, he runs around the car, opening my door, and I rush out.

Falling to my hands and knees on the gritty dirt, I heave and choke up my stomach until my throat is raw and burning from the bile, my eyes watering. I feel Rik's hand on my back, rubbing small circles, trying to soothe me.

When the feeling passes, I slowly stand with Rik's help, wobbling on my feet. His stormy-blue eyes meet mine in the dimly lit darkness as he moves a strand of my hair out of my face.

"You did it. He's gone," he softly reassures me.

I feel the tears welling in my eyes as I realize he is right. The weight of the last two years is slowly being lifted away as an intense relief washes over me.

I stare into his eyes, smiling, feeling light as a feather.

"I am finally free," I say breathlessly. "I can finally live my life without having to fear him anymore."

With the monsters of my past gone, I can't wait to see what life has to offer.

The end... or is it?

ACKNOWLEDGEMENTS

I'm thrilled to share a little about the wonderful people who have made my journey as a writer possible. Writing my book has been a spiral of emotions, and I couldn't have done it without the incredible support of my husband, David. He has been my rock, always encouraging me to chase my dreams and reminding me to never give up—thank you, hon! I love you to the moon and back.

Family has always been my strength and backbone. My mother, Amanda, may you rest in peace; you are my guiding star in the dark. To my father, Yancy, who taught me that dreaming is the first step to achieving, and to my grandparents, aunts, uncles, and my amazing sisters—Courtney, Caitlyn, Helen—as well as my wonderful sister-in-laws, Gloria and Alexandra, you all have cheered me on every step of making this dream come true. And to my new step-mom, Rebekah, your support and listening ear during tough times have meant the world to me. (Hope I don't make y'all blush too bad, sorry in advance. And please don't look at me any differently.)

I'm also blessed to be the mother of two wonderful kids who inspire me daily. I want you both to know that anything is possible if you put your mind to it—never stop trying!

A heartfelt shout-out to my friends—Misty, Kate, Nick, Luis, my brother-in-law Aaron, and my sister Courtney—your feedback and playful banter provided just the right motivation to keep me going.

Violet S.R. Cox

 I owe a special thanks to Cody Gartlan, who sparked the initial idea for this book during an unforgettable late-night chat over a decade ago; your creativity still inspires me!

 I'd be remiss if I didn't mention the talented Mehreen, my book cover designer, who turned my vision into a remarkable reality, and of course, the fabulous Michaela, my editor, whose keen eye for detail turned my manuscript into the polished piece it is today. Thank you for joining me on this journey.

THANK YOU!

Thank you for going on this adventure with Selen. I hope you enjoyed Sweet Vengeance. Please tells spread the word about this book if you enjoyed and leave reviews. I greatly appreciate it.

You are welcome to follow me on social media.

TikTok: *@violetsrcox*

Facebook: *@violet.s.r.cox*

About the Author

    Violet S.R. Cox is an aspiring writer and dedicated family woman from the charming town of Beaufort, South Carolina, where she continues to reside with her husband and two children—a son and a daughter. Raised by her hardworking parents, Amanda and Yancy, who are respected local handymen, Violet learned the importance of dedication and perseverance from a young age. Her passion for writing blossomed during her middle school years, providing an outlet for her vivid imagination and creative expression. An early graduate of Beaufort High School, class of 2013, Violet distinguished herself both academically and personally, often seen with notebooks in hand to capture her thoughts and ideas. Beyond her writing pursuits, she cherishes quality time with her family, fully embracing the joys of motherhood. In addition to her literary interests, Violet enjoys playing pool as a member of her local pool team, showcasing her competitive spirit. With a commitment to both her craft and her family, Violet S.R. Cox continues to inspire those around her. Her unique blend of creativity and dedication drives her to explore new ideas and stories, shaping her journey as a writer and a mother in the heart of Beaufort.

Violet S.R. Cox

Made in the USA
Columbia, SC
09 August 2024

48beefdb-39b1-4db8-9a93-a9698b2ffa16R01